'Twixt the sun and the moon, dream and reality fuse until the man, in his sleep, dreams he is a butterfly. On waking-up, can he be sure he isn't a butterfly dreaming he is a man . . . ?

A GUEST ROOM DIGEST

Most, not all, these little short stories are based on "Happenings" to either friends, or ourselves.

Albine Taylor

A GUEST ROOM DIGEST

Albine Taylor

The Book Guild Ltd
Sussex, England

First published in Great Britain in 2003 by
The Book Guild Ltd,
25 High Street,
Lewes, East Sussex
BN7 2LU

Typesetting in Baskerville by
IML Typographers, Birkenhead, Merseyside

Printed in Great Britain by
Bookcraft (Bath) Ltd, Avon

A catalogue record for this book is available from
The British Library

ISBN 1 85776 649 0

CONTENTS

1

What's in a Breed

'What about a cup of coffee?' suggested my husband as we reached a small seaside town in Belgium.

It was a charming, though noisy, little café and it smelled deliciously of freshly ground coffee. It struck me I might try to find out if anyone bred my favourite breed of dogs here. After all, this was the country of origin of the papillon.

'Anything else?' asked the waitress taking our order.

'Yes,' I chipped in, 'could you tell me if anyone around here breeds papillons?'

'What?' stuttered the amazed waitress.

'Tiny little dogs with beautiful big ears like butterflies' wings,' I volunteered. 'And they have long bushy tails.'

Obviously more used to handling cups of coffee than dogs, the poor woman drew in her breath, making a hissing sound.

'Well, there is a lady in the next road breeds dozens of small dogs.' She gave me the address.

'Dogs!' spat the lady of the house, 'Certainly not ... But there is a woman in the next avenue that does ...'

'Please,' I enquired in the next avenue, 'do you happen to breed papillons?'

'Ah! You mean those funny little dogs like door mats! *Oui*?'

'*Non*,' I interrupted, horrified. '*Petits Papillons* ... Lovely little dogs, *avec* big ears and gay bushy tails...'

'*Très bien. Là*, there, across the road, she has dogs. Oh la la! *Beaucoup beaucoup*... Many dogs!'

When we got inside the house it smelled as if it hadn't had an open window in months

'It certainly doesn't smell very butterflyish!' complained my husband.

'No,' I agreed, 'more like long wet hair. Spaniel, or peke,' I said.

A shuffling across the hall accompanied by squeaks heralded our hostess. She entered surrounded by half a dozen excited pekes.

I introduced myself. '...And I am looking for a papillon breeder.'

'Oh la la! *Non, non.* I breed *Pekinois*, see, are they not beautiful?'

'Yes, quite,' I agreed absentmindedly. 'I'm sorry to have troubled you, *Madame. Merci...*'

'Oh! No, no, don't go. Let me show you Tina. She really is very beautiful, don't you think?'

Before I could argue, Tina's good points were pointed out to me. I was handed a couple of her puppies, and given a practical demonstration on how to arrange a whelping basket. After a detailed account of first aid procedure for new-born pups who look more fit for a mini grave, I found myself agreeing that ... 'Yes, they are very lovely pups ... But ... Yes, quite, Tina should do very well in the show ring ... But ... I am very sorry, I want a papillon...'

'All right, I will make enquiries for you. Give me your

name and address and I will let you know as soon as I have some names for you.'

'Thank you very much, that's most kind of you,' I said gratefully, relieved she was not going to press me to take one of her puppies.

'I hope you like my little dogs. Yes?' she asked.

'Very much, though I must admit I've never been fond of pekes . . .'

'Ah! I was just like you. I didn't like them at all,' she cried.

I gasped in astonishment. 'Then what made you breed them?'

'Well, my present husband's daughter bred them before I met him. She had prize-winning dogs. One day she came to see me to tell me she had fallen in love with my husband, would I exchange him for her prize-winning champions?' She chuckled seeing my bewildered expression. 'And I said yes. That's how I started . . . I was fed up with him anyway, and I had the best part of the bargain because I married her father and bred winning dogs whereas she soon got tired of my ex-husband and divorced him within a year!' She smiled at me as we shook hands and said: 'I'm sorry I have no papillons for you.'

'Please don't worry!' I smiled back. 'I wouldn't dream of exchanging my husband, even for a papillon!'

Back in the car we had a good laugh, in spite of not finding what we were seeking. 'At least you've got yourself a good story!' said my husband philosophically.

2

My Cooker and I

'How marvellous to have fresh vegetables! And new-laid eggs...'

'You are lucky to have such a view!...'

'You are lucky to live in the country...!'

Lucky! Have my town sisters ever thought about the work one puts into making a home? It doesn't just grow, nor do the vegetables ... without a lot of work and effort. Paradoxically their expression of pity when they remark: 'Don't you get bored, my dear? What ever do you find to do all day?' Makes me wonder, at times, if we belong to the same human race.

When we bought this derelict old farmhouse, it had been on the market for months, spurned by everyone. It had no water, gas, electricity, sanitation, drains, telephone ... But it had a view!

Raising a family under those conditions as well as doing the building ourselves belongs to another story. Water had to be pumped up and it required a mathematical problem to put it to its best use without wasting a drop!

Method is all-important; forget to trim your wick, or fill the oil lamps, or place the matches always in exactly the same place, and then try to find your way in the dark if you should come home late, or in an emergency!

Forethought is top of the list if you are to make a successful country housewife. There is no 'Meal in a jiffy' – 'Turn on the hot-plate' or 'Use regulo no. 4 . . .' If you want to cook dinner at 6 p.m. it's in the morning you have to make the necessary preparations.

A solid-fuel cooker provides you with warmth, essential in old stone-floored houses, hot water around the clock, and a constant oven, providing you have planned ahead! Otherwise you cook as I used to do, when it reached the right temperature (usually much too late, or too early . . . Seldom when I *had* to cook). There is no mystique about it, just planning, stoking up at the right time controlling the flues, riddling the ashes. Fresh black coal, especially when damp with mist or frost, will drop the temperature of both your oven and your hot-plate. It takes several hours to have a steady red glow producing its maximum output of heat.

Now we have a woodburning cooker, a Franco-Belge, and it is excellent, responding almost instantly. From cold, it will boil a kettle in ten minutes when lit with dry wood.

What is there to do? When told there is only one bus a week, visitors cry: 'Don't you miss the shops? – Questions obviously not answered to their satisfaction when I assure them that we are almost self-supporting, and that nowhere else would you get such service but in the country. From the oil-man to the haberdasheries, everything comes to your doorstep.

Entertainment? 'Don't you miss the theatre, the films?'

I have a permanent film show in technicolour; every morning as I look out of my window I see completely new scenery. The green hills roll out into the distance across the valley, mysteriously shrouded in mist, or coyly hiding behind a curtain of rain, or smiling through streaks of sunshine dappled with the shadows of countless leaves of differing shades of greens. A large dog-fox suns himself in the dip by the goat house. A pheasant struts across the lawn. Numerous creatures and alternating shapes and colours, different moods with an inexhaustible supply of lighting effects, make every day feel new, fresh, and exciting. The birds' chorus, the pearly dew-clad cobwebs, the variety of scents from the crisp cool grass with a touch of frost or the warm damp earth in the mellow coppery light of autumn and the fruity smells of summer, never fail to stimulate me. Unlike watching a film passively, enjoying the country involves all your senses.

Peace? – Yes, but for those of us who *live* in the country it is very different from the weekender's notion of peace and quiet.

After the mad rush and the commotion of breakfast, complicated at times by a luke-warm hot-plate incapable of frying, there is the milking. Oh yes, we have goats and they provide us with our butter and cheese as well as milk. The poultry has to be let out, the eggs collected, the feed and water troughs filled. I pull up a few weeds as I go along, not that anyone will notice the difference, there are too many, and quickly glance at the vegetable plot. Pigeons ravage the rows of peas, cats dig up seed beds, slugs halve the lettuce crop... Frost kills off young buds on the fruit trees, moles cause their own brand of destruction. You can always be assured of finding something ... when you look at your vegetable plot! And jobs mount up, all necessary, but some more urgent than others. Then it's a toss-up between gardening, mucking out, or making the beds, washing the kitchen floor, unrecognisable under a criss-cross of paws and footmarks...

With luck, if good management has failed, I sit down to a chunk of cheese and steaming hot coffee at lunch time, but three pairs of eyes stare accusingly at me and there is nothing for it but to get back into boots and mac, and trample across the fields with the dogs. Returning, not in time for tea, but to fill up the hayracks with freshly cut greens for the goats and rabbits. In rainy weather those reproachful eyes follow my progress as I redecorate, or do some repairs, in a silence unrepentant for their suppressed impatience at being confined.

Suddenly it's time to collect the children from school. A glance at my cooker confirms my fear, I forgot to riddle or fill up ... I open the flues and hope it'll be all right by the time I get back. Tea-time is a downpour of woes, broken friendships, new ones, sorrows and triumphs, then it's all hands on deck for a last round of feeding and locking up, in the winter, or a swim in our home-made pool in the summer. As relative peace descends upon heads bowed over homework, I get started on preparing the dinner.

This is my moment of triumph, if I have managed my cooker properly, or my undoing, if I forgot ... Everything is home produced, from the duckling (hopefully) cooking in the oven, to the apples in the sauce, and forgotten is the mud and the soaking I got collecting the vegetables earlier in the day.

The day I have a dozen ducks or hens to kill and pluck invariably seems to attract the most finicky of our friends, and I try hard to smile welcomingly through a cloud of feathers and down clinging to my face and hair, extending an elbow to shake as my hands bear the stamp of my bloody deeds, and they (the visitors) pinch their noses imperceptibly at the smells unfamiliar to them.

That is all in the course of a *day*. Evening allows for

7

relaxation and hobbies. As I sit scanning through seed catalogues, planning the following season's work, I try not to worry about the carpet under a mound of patterns and scraps of materials and the large tailoring scissors whose jaws seemingly want to chop their way through anything in sight. The large dining table has temporarily disappeared under a collection of stamps or coins, or both. Barely an hour seems to have passed since the room was tidy! The radio entertains us all, but there is no battery-run TV. Amazingly, we are all busy, and I think contented, maybe just ignorant of what we are missing?

It took us 18 months to hack our way through the brambles and nettles before we discovered a delightful pond, now a feature of the garden where our saplings have grown into handsome trees and bold groups of shrubs hide patches of flowers, affording our visitors pleasant surprises as they stroll round. We can offer them a swim during hot days, or putting on our sons' putting green, even practice bunker shots! We can entertain their children in our pets' corner, where rabbits, tortoises, doves, cats and dogs all co-habit happily. They can gather fruit from the orchard, feed the ducks on the pond, or sit in the rose arbour sipping home-made wines. In the winter a log fire mellows them. We can offer them most things, but ... I cannot offer them a meal-in-a-jiffy! My stubborn old cooker won't co-operate, forcing me to use ingenuity, imagination, and foresight. Yet nothing in the world would make me part with it. As my drooling sisters return to their cities their words echo pleasantly, in my ears: 'How lucky you are!' ... And the mud and the dirt and the old water pump surround me ... 'Such views!' ... Ah, yes, we really *are* lucky.

And in the dead of night I can sit in my cosy kitchen, thanks to my old cooker, and indulge in my own hobbies: pottery, writing, or basket making. Cosy and snug, when only the owls call . . .

3

The Nymphs of the Lake

The water-lilies go
To and fro
Rocking in the ripples of the water,
Lazy on a leaf lies the Lake King's daughter,
And the faint winds shake her.
Who will come and take her?
I will, I will!
Keep still! Keep still!
Sleeping on a leaf lies the Lake King's Daughter....
Then the winds come skipping
To the lilies on the water;
And the kind winds wake her.
Now who will take her?
With a laugh she is slipping
Through the lilies on the water.
Wait! Wait!
Too late, too late!
Only the water-lilies go
To and fro
Dipping, dipping,
To the ripples of the water.

(*A.A. Milne*)

Nymphea Odorata, the sweet-scented Lake King's daughter, whom we fondly called Nina for short, never fails to sit among the giant lilies in the pond where the sun and the moon in turn caress her with their shimmering rays.

'Lazy on a leaf lies the Lake King's daughter . . .'

And none have ever told a mortal soul how she stayed there, lovely, and proud. It all began a long time ago when Nina first wanted to see the sun and feel its warmth, or sit and play with the silvery moonbeams.

'Father dear,' coaxed Nina softly as her father rested from his duties, 'I wish I could go to the surface of the pond and sit in the warm sunshine . . .'

'But, dearest daughter, is not our water garden the most beautiful home a nymph could wish for?' exclaimed the King, a little worried that his favourite daughter seemed unhappy.

'Yes, father dear,' replied Nina quickly, 'but we never see a sunray nor a moonbeam . . .'

'Indeed we do! In the loveliest patterns no mortal has ever seen. They try so hard to swim to our regions with masks and oxygen cylinders just to catch a glimpse of our treasures and enjoy the way the ripples of the water break up those rays into thousands of patterns.'

'I know, father, but likewise I would like to see a straight shaft of light.' She fondly caressed the weeds from around his throne. 'Please let me go to the surface?' she pleaded with persuasive charm.

'Oh well,' said the King, unable to resist his daughter, 'go, my dear, but be very careful no mortal sees you, or you will become a mortal yourself!'

'I'd sooner be a water-lily!' reassured Nina. 'I couldn't

11

be parted from you, father dear, and at least my roots would be near you forever.'

As she glided gracefully to the top of the lily pond, we, the young nymphs, all swam with her. She peeped through the leaves and smelt the sweet scented air and cried out: 'How lovely and warm it is!' Her enthusiasm rippled through us as she climbed on to a leaf, and we danced just below the surface keeping her afloat whilst: *'Lazy on the leaf lay the Lake King's daughter...'*

But soon the sun rose above the tall trees of the forest, and the heat was too much for Nina, so she slipped through the lilies of the water.

'It was too hot!' she confessed to her father when she returned. 'But I will try again, when the moon shines...'

As soon as the moon was full Nina once more swam to the top of the lily pond, and all the young nymphs followed her, dancing merrily just below the leaves to support them whilst *'Lazy on the leaf lay the Lake King's daughter...'* She gazed around her in wonder.

'This is more beautiful than I imagined!' She sang the words and the sound of her voice whispering through the trees pleased her.

She sat on the lily pads singing in the moonbeam until the moon slowly disappeared behind the trees, just before the sun rose, and the moon called out: 'Sun, oh sun! When you reach the lily pond in the middle of the forest, you will see a most beautiful creature with a voice like crystal bells.'

When the sun was high enough it glared down at the lily pond, but Nina was already slipping through the lilies of the water.

'The moonbeams were wonderful, but the sunshine is too hot for me...' she complained to her father when she returned to his palace of weeds.

'Why not get one of the nymphs to bring an urn, and pour water over you,' he suggested half-heartedly, but always ready to satisfy her wishes.

Once more Nina swam to the top of the lily pond, and as the young mymphs danced to keep her afloat I climbed on the lily pad with her, keeping a trickle of water glistening over her lovely smooth body. But, alas, as the sun rose above the trees and the scents of the forest became heady and strong with the heat, I could stand it no longer, and slipped back through the ripples of the water as she took the urn from me.

Her voice rang out merrily as she sang and laughed, amused with catching the sun's rays, turning them into prisms as the tiny pearls of water clothed her like a jeweled garment. So absorbed was she in these new delights, she never heard our warning until it was too late. The young Mortal stood in the shade of the trees lining the mossy bank.

'Who are you?' he asked. 'You are more beautiful than the pink blossoms of the water-lilies. . . .'

Nina dropped the urn in surprise but before she could answer the heat made her faint.

We fled for our lives as the handsome young Mortal dived into the lake to save her and when he had successfully brought her to the mossy bank beneath the tall trees I cautiously peeped out and saw him gaze at her, stroking her gently until she opened her eyes. There was a light in them I had never seen before . . . a new softness, and she smiled . . .

'Nina! Nina! Come back . . .' I cried in vain as all the young nymphs returned weeping to the King's garden.

She sprang to her feet when she heard me and ran back to the water, but the young Mortal caught her by the arm.

13

'Let me go!' she cried. 'Let me go back to my father...'

As she stepped on to the lily pads they no longer supported her and she slowly sank through the ripples of the water, the young Mortal's cries ringing in her ears: 'Come back, my sweet blossom! Come back...'

I watched, spellbound, as her heart broke, and the fruit of her love blossomed in a sweet-scented lily which floated gracefully to the edge of the pond to collect her lover's tears as he knelt disconsolate on the bank.

Down through the ages of human time *Nymphea odorata* is the only sweet-scented water-lily, and no one knows the sorrow cupped in its heart as it nurses those tears. Her roots are close to her father's garden as she lies among the other lilies, and the sun and the moon take it in turns to caress her. Yet, the love she bore triumphs over the spell, and should you be lucky enough to be there when the moon is full, or the sun shines through the rain, you might, for a brief moment, catch a glimpse of Nina as she sits on the lily leaves and we, the young nymphs, dance briefly just below the surface of the water. For a brief moment and then, '*With a laugh she is slipping through the lilies of the water...*' And there, where you saw her but a moment ago, you will see the beautiful scented water-lily *Nymphea odorata*, and:

> Only the water-lilies go
> To and fro
> Dipping, dipping,
> To the ripples of the water.

But I cannot tell you where the Lake King's pond is to be

14

found. The secret awaits for the insight of eyes unclouded by longing. Those who are bound by desire see only the outward container...

4

Shanghai, May 1925

'So this is Shanghai!' I exclaimed. 'I don't like it very much,' I said with all the conviction of my eight years' knowledge of the world.

'Well, I can't go any further, I have had enough walking...' coughed Shan, my little companion.

I stared at my friend, and suddenly saw the great change which had come over him since we had left home after the war-lords had destroyed our village. Shan had always been thin, but now his eyes were shining unusually brightly from deep sunken sockets and there was even less flesh on his thin bones. Every rib stood out as he bent over in a fit of violent coughing.

'We could stay here for a while until you get better,' I suggested, 'then we can go on with our journey. I wish we had stayed in Peking ... it was so lovely there ...'

'I don't. It was in Peking that I started this coughing. The camel man said all that dust came from the Gobi desert. I wonder why it did not affect you!'

We were two small boys dragging ourselves wearily through the slummy outskirts before finally finding a disused shed. Here Shan lay exhausted in the far corner, and fell into a restless sleep. I dozed for a while before the usual pangs of hunger sent me out in search of food

16

as the afternoon sun beat down. There was little garbage at this time of the day, others had passed earlier ... And as I stared at the blank lethargic men making their way through the dusty earth-trodden alleys, I wondered where help could be sought from ... The people looked like miserable skeletons, not unlike Shan. Their dwellings were made of dried mud around which dirty naked babies played, watched over by ancient shaggy old women. The smell was that of decomposition, a mixture of sweat, rotting garbage, and urine.

I had no idea how long I wandered aimlessly, but the sun was setting by the time I reached the waterside.

The activities and the noisy lively chatter of the men on the wharf contrasted with the morbid apathy of the slums. The salty air stung my nostrils pleasantly and I breathed deeply, filling my lungs with its exhilarating powers. As I sat on a coil of rope, I watched the lights come on one by one, immediately throwing themselves in the perpetual motion of the waters. The men had left, and at last I was alone, my mind racing like the thousand ripples that danced in and out of the pools of light.

'And what may one so small be thinking about at this time of night?'

I shot off the coil of rope, grazing my leg, but unaware of the pain in my fright.

'I am sorry if I scared you. But it is very late for you to be out alone, little one ...'

I looked up at the kindly wrinkled old face. Each wrinkle caught the light reflected from the water, making a weird mask of deep well-defined strips of light and shade. The old man sat down on the coil I had just vacated and smiled broadly; his white teeth flashed and his eyes creased into slits from which two sparks twinkled now and again.

17

'Don't be afraid,' he insisted. 'I only wondered if you were lost. Shanghai is a very large place!'

'Thank you no. I am not lost I was only looking for food.'

'At this hour? What about your parents?'

'We have none. We've just arrived ... We don't know where to go.'

'Who is "we"?' The old mask of light and shade never ceased to smile. It was as if it were permanently set like a plaster cast.

'Shan and me. I left him in a shed, he is very ill...'

'Have you come a long way?'

'From Liang Ts'un – a long way. Up in the mountains.'

'I know it well. I lived there once.' The old man shivered slightly as if in memory of the cold mountains, and tucked his hands up the sleeves of his old faded blue robe. 'If you lead me to your little friend I can take you both to my home. It is only a humble mud hut, but then an old one like myself does not need very much!' The old man's grin flashed broader than ever. 'You are welcome to stay as long as you like.'

I was stunned at first. Though we had met with kindness on our way, we had never been asked inside. At most we were offered to bed down in the straw with the animals. More often than not we had to huddle together at the foot of a wall for shelter.

'Come now, little one, let's find Shan.' The old man rose, putting a hand on his back as if to help himself up. He straightened, still smiling. 'I am getting old!' he conceded, shaking his head.

The mud hut was spotlessly clean. The beaten earth floor smelled sweet like the earth of the country, the hole which acted as window was covered with a sheet of waxed paper, the straw mat was fresh. I felt over-whelmed with a sense of peace in this unexpected and most welcome harbour. I watched silently as the old man laid Shan gently on his straw mat and covered him over with a faded blue quilt.

'And now,' smiled our benefactor, 'we will have some-thing hot to eat and drink.'

With great economy of movement he organised the evening meal, the stillness being interrupted only by Shan's coughing. Gradually I felt sleep invade me. I had not known how tired I was till now, but as the whiffs from the cooking pot tickled my nostrils I sat cross-legged on the floor, my head held high like a light-house dominating a sea of drowsiness, and as my eyes tried to close I forced them open each time a little more.

In the dim light I saw the bowl of steaming hot rice held out to me and took it automatically, my fingers coming into contact with the old man's cold and knot-ted hands. Silently we smiled at each other.

'My name is Yang. What is yours, little one?' he enquired softly.

'Lin,' I answered.

As daylight trickled through the waxed paper window I seemed to see the old man for the first time. He was still tall, with a slight stoop of the shoulders. He wore a faded tunic of coarse blue cloth fastened up the front with loops of silk and strips of knotted silk for buttons. A round black cap came down to his forehead, covering what hair he had.

'I will go and look for work,' I announced, getting up. 'We will need medicine for Shan ... And we have to pay you back for your kindness.'

19

Old Yang shook his head and waved the sentence aside. But a moment later he nodded his head and conceded: 'We will need medicine to make him comfortable till the end.'

I stared at the sleeping figure of my companion, then at old Yang.

'Shan die?' I questioned, horrified. 'But he has had so little time, and we have nothing to give him for his journey.'

'He won't need anything, once he is with God.'

'But the gods themselves need so much!' I persisted. 'And it will be for his journey ... He will need food and...'

Old Yang shook his head and interrupted. 'He won't need anything, I tell you.'

'I have seen funeral processions.' I protested.

'Ssh! Don't argue or you will wake him. Now leave all these things to me, like a good boy.'

I found work in the mills in the British concession, and I hated every minute of it. I tried my best to please the difficult foreman, who thought nothing of thrashing us if he suspected we were idling. I knew that however small the payment, it was vital for Shan's comfort. I could not help but feel pleased that he was too ill to work in this dreadful place where men were little more than beavers working away in their dark holes.

I squatted in a dark corner and was stealing a few minutes' rest when I overheard hushed voices. I listened, and peeping through a crack in the wooden partition watched a group of haggard men, heads close together in a conspirational huddle.

'And,' said the oldest one in low tones, 'we have the students on our side ...'

'It is indeed time that something was done to stop these foreigners from disregarding Chiang's orders...'

'He at least wants to put a stop to child labour!' agreed a tall thin youth in a high-pitched voice. 'The only decent thing he's done...'

They all nodded their heads. 'We must meet after work and make plans.'

'Yes, yes...' the others chorused. 'We must talk it over with the students and get something organised.'

Suddenly there was an angry roar as the foreman entered the room.

'Break it up! Break it up! Get on with your work, you lazy good for nothing scum ... What are you plotting now?'

The little group scattered, scurrying back to their respective places like a lot of frightened mice in the presence of a particularly vicious cat.

'What do you make of it?' asked one of my little companions on the way home.

'I don't know, who is this Chiang?'

'He is trying to build a new and united China, and free us from the foreigners...'

'That's right,' cut in the tall thin youth with the falsetto voice. 'But it is not easy, there are many difficulties and many enemies. It takes a good and careful captain to steer a ship safely around a rocky coast and avoid all the pitfalls...'

'But my father says that all paths lead to the top of the mountains, persisted my first companion. 'And anyway, the government can't agree, and there's too many warlords!'

'Maybe, but some paths are safer than others, if a little slower.'

'Is this Chiang a careful captain then?' I asked at last.

'Well, little one, he is the only leader we have at the moment capable of freeing us from the foreigners and unfair treaties. He is *not* our choice ... his task is not an easy one and there is much intervention. I suppose history may tell, but right now run along home and leave these problems for older heads to bear...' He smiled kindly at us before going on his way.

'Let's have a race!' I suggested, wanting to dispel the gloom which had descended upon my companions. I had no interest in politics and did not understand them, nor why they affected my companions so. 'I'll run and hide, see if you can find me ...'

I had almost lost them from sight when I heard them shouting after me, but there was a park ahead and I knew I'd find plenty of hiding places there. As I darted among the trees, one of those foreign ladies shouted at me, then turned to an enormous man with red hair and bristling whiskers. His face went quite red as he picked me up by my collar and shook me, rather like a terrier shakes a rat.

'You filthy little bastard! How dare you come into this park? Did you not read the notices?' Turning to his wife, he added, 'Call the police.' The giant raised his stick and brought it down on my back. The pain brought tears to my eyes, which burned as they momentarily stayed on the brim of my eyelids, magnifying this hateful foreign devil. I stood staring at him, hating him, and clenching my fists till I could feel my nails digging into the palms of my hands.

'You insolent little beggar!' raged the giant as I did not move away. 'So you defy me? I'll show you ...' He raised his stick again, but still I did not move. He fully expected me to run away and miscalculated his stroke. The stick hit the ground a few inches from where I stood, and snapped in two.

His face went purple, and I felt sure it would burst, but I did not stay to find out. I turned and fled. Outside, the other children waited for me, huddled together, looking terrified.

'You should not have gone in there!' they cried. 'That is one of the parks reserved for the foreigners! the notice says "no dogs or Chinese allowed!"'

'How was I to know?' I demanded irritably. 'Anyway, why should they stop us? We are in our own country!' I found myself repeating words I had heard that afternoon in the mill. They had meant nothing to me then, but now they inflamed me rather like a festering wound inflames the flesh around it. 'Why don't they go back to their own land? China is a free country and belongs to us.'

'Come on, Lin,' they implored as they dragged me away. 'Let's get home before the police get here...'

I might have gone on feeling sore about it, if old Yang had not greeted me on the doorstep with the fateful words: 'Shan has left us. He died a short time ago...'

I forgot about the foreigners, the park, the men's talk at the mill, and followed Yang into the hut feeling suddenly docile and subdued.

But on the day of the demonstration, that May 1925, my curiosity took the better of me and drove me to the heart of the trouble. I felt strangely lost in this surging sea of unknown faces, and when I tried to get out of it, I found I had become imprisoned by it. There was nothing I could do about it now, caught up as I was in the current which swept through Shanghai. I wished in vain that I had obeyed Yang and stayed at home ... My longing for adventure and my curiosity had been stronger than my sense of duty...

We reached a cordon of police who, wielding their clubs, broke in on the crowd, hitting indiscriminately, but in vain. They were unable to stop the wave, which rolled on unheeding with ever-increasing determination.

There was a moment's lull before the air vibrated and exploded. Panic seized the crowd as firing broke out. The smell of gunpowder clung heavily to the cloud of smoke which now enveloped the scene and muffled the cries of the demonstrators as they were being ruthlessly mown down. Too petrified to move, I lay between two fallen bodies for what seemed ages. The noise gradually died down and the crowd vanished; only the smoke and the smell remained ... the hot smell of bodies and sweat, of gunpowder and blood, of terror and tears. The mixture was acrid and bitter as it caught at my throat.

I rose after a while and crawled to the shelter of a wall. I could see someone coming towards me.

'Yang! Yang!' I called out hoarsely as I watched him coming closer, unable to move from my shelter. There was no smile of recognition on his wrinkled old face. And in this tense moment I reflected that it was the first time I had seen the old man frown.

'I found the hut empty, and knew where to find you...' There was pain in his voice as he reprimanded me. 'I told you to stay indoors...'

I tried to find some suitable words of apology, but just then a police patrol fired a last defiant shot.

It was a few moments before Yang sank slowly to his knees and without a murmur rolled over and lay still on the ground. I threw myself on his body, my face close to his in the hope that he would hear me. My tears ran down the grooves of his wrinkled old face as his faded old eyes turned glassy and unseeing. It was too late to find words of apology, Yang would never hear them now...

Once again the sun was setting, casting its last pale light, leaving me alone, weary, and bewildered.

5

The Inheritance

Break, Break, Break,
   On thy cold gray stones, O Sea!
And I would that my tongue could utter
   The thoughts that arise in me.

O, well for the fisherman's boy,
   That he shouts with his sister at play!
O, well for the sailor lad,
   That he sings in his boat on the bay!

And the stately ships go on
   To their haven under the hill;'
But O for the touch of a vandish'd hand,
   And the sound of a voice that is still!

Break, break, break
   At the foot of thy crags, O Sea!
But the tender grace of a day that is dead
   Will never come back to me.

              Alfred Lord Tennyson

The seagulls wheeled round, making full use of the sea breeze to carry them up into the grey sky, disappearing suddenly over the tops of the jagged cliffs until their cries alone were left to echo from the crags.

'We're in for a storm, best make for home,' stated Meredith, raising his voice as the fishing boat's engine chugged raspingly.

'There's plenty of time, father. We've just hit a good spot.'

Meredith knocked the ash from his pipe and stuffed it into his pocket before returning to the wheelhouse to check their position. The light from his small grey eyes had to fight through the shade of his thick bristly eyebrows as he frowned. He wiped the salt spray out of his greying ginger beard with a slow rounded movement of his darkly burned hand and turned thoughtfully to survey the young man at the wheel.

'James wants a little longer . . .' he started uncertainly, watching for the reaction which would give him a clue to the young man's thoughts. 'How about it, Toni?'

'Best make for home.' Toni's voice sounded calculatingly casual, and his eyes remained glued to the open space where the sky and the sea merged into an ominous dark stain. 'The winds are veering to gale force. ' His fingers tightened round the wheel until his knuckles showed white, but there was no change in his voice as he threw back his head and spoke to the old man squatting in the far corner of the cabin. 'Bit risky, Moby?'

'Och, man, what does James ken aboot the sea! Toni's richt, if we don't turrn back noo we'll ha'e a hard time. . .' He spared a quick, furtive glance at Meredith through his small slits of flint, and his contempt rolled, enriched by his Scottish accent. 'These city tycoons make me sick! They go yachting and fishing at weekends. Bah! They play at it, but what do they ken aboot it, as a way of life?'

27

'He has to make a start somewhere, Moby,' Meredith said, too quickly to be convincing. For a moment he watched the old deck-hand roll his tobacco carefully between oil-grimy fingers before licking the paper and tidying the ends of his newly made cigarette. The responsibility was his. He owed this old man no explanations. 'Be fair, you old rogue,' he tried to laugh. 'Break him in gradually. Give him his head just a little ...'

He could feel Moby's steely eyes watching with the rapaciousness of a hawk and the patience of a vulture as he struck the match. But its light only revealed the deep grooves of the old man's chiselled features.

'I'll take the wheel, Toni. Go and get the nets in. And, Toni, check the rigging. Oh, and make sure the gear is safe ...' Meredith was about to find Toni another job, but the young man, having fastened his oilskins, had left the comparative shelter of the wheelhouse without a word. He braced himself and, bending into the wind, walked, sure-footed, across the slippery deck of his father's boat.

'Don't be such an old woman!' chided James, trying to release his brother's hold on the net. 'Heavens, man, a little rain and wind shouldn't frighten you! I thought the sea was in your veins.'

'Ever been at sea in a gale?'

'You're chicken!'

But Toni was shouting instructions, and his sharp, cutting voice allowed no room for doubt as to who was in command. When the small catch was disgorged, Toni ordered with controlled calm: 'Get out of the way whilst I lash the gear before the storm breaks.' He pushed past James and, as they collided, James was made fully aware of his brother's suppressed anger.

'Beats me why you wanted to come. You never showed any interest before ... Too busy making your fortune in

28

London!' A vicious light shone from his eyes as he squinted into the wind. 'What happened to it?' He paused, seemingly waiting for a lull in the howling through the rigging, and a sudden short break in the clouds allowed the reddening sun to cast a surreptious metallic light to illuminate the angry young features which glistened under a coating of salt water. 'This is *my* life, James. Not yours,' Toni ended.

'All right, so I was out of work . . . But it is father's business,' mocked James. But seeing the signs of battle in his young brother's clenched fists he felt it more expedient to retire from the deck.

At the wheelhouse he tried again.

'Why not let the nets drag? After all, we might catch something on the way home,' he persisted.

'We'll have enough to do,' snapped Meredith through the smoke of his pipe. 'Ever been at sea in a gale ? Needs a strong stomach. Rocky coast – tricky.'

'Why not make for the open sea then?'

'Not an ocean-going liner.' Meredith's face seemed to crease until it looked as hard set as his cryptic sentences.

'Well, dash it, she *is* seaworthy, I take it?'

'Aye, lad, she is that. For what she was built, that is. Not for yer fanciful ideas though.' He turned his weathered eyes away from the sea to stare hard and meaningfully at his ambitious son, and missed Toni's frantic signals.

James ignored them too, as he ignored his father's remark. Digging his hands deep into his pockets, he played idly with the contents before leaning nonchalantly against the glass pane, effectively cutting Toni out of sight.

'Ach, I'll be on my way noo, Meredith.' Old Moby never could stand the sound of jingling coins. 'Got better things to do than listen to a lay-aboot.' He readjusted his moth-eaten old favourite, patting the red pompom to ensure it was well anchored to his balding head. 'Ye'll live to regret this, Meredith. Toni's the boy. Slaves all day long on this hulk and it's Toni fetch this, Toni do that, Toni fetch, Toni carry ... Toni, Meredith, knows his trade like the fish swim the seas!' The storm clouds seemed gathered in old Moby's eyes as he cast them a last contemptuous glance.

'Crappy old man!' scoffed James after he'd left. 'Beats me why you keep him on. Looks a bit past it to me. All told, this is a most inefficient way of making a living. What you want to do is expand! Get bigger boats, instead of these short trips in and out with small catches. It's antiquated, nowadays you need to think big.'

Meredith felt like hitting out, but refrained from even glancing at James. All these years I've tried to be patient. I mustn't lose my temper now he thought. Aloud, he snapped curtly, 'Get off yer arse and help Toni lash the canvas.'

The deck was awash and slippery. After a few faltering steps, James grabbed the nearest thing to hand. His feet slipped from under him and he tightened his hold on the rope, hanging on to it for dear life.

'You fool!' Toni's voice seemed hurled at him with all the viciousness of the howling gale. 'You've just undone all my work by pulling that knot!'

The canvas tore from its loosened anchorage, and with a thunderous clap first wrapped itself round the wheelhouse before making a hysterical flight to the top of the mast, where it flapped like a horde of possessed Dervishes.

Meredith left the wheelhouse to rush to Toni's help as the riotous gear reeled drunkenly across the deck, charging at the trapped young man.

'Watch it!' cried James as the full force of the maddened canvas defeated the mast's stoic stand and a tearing screech came from its base. 'All hands on deck!' he called down to the hold where the crew sorted out the fish.

'Bit late, mate!' they snapped as they pushed him aside.

The mast came down so slowly as James watched it with fascinated horror that he missed seeing the huge wave which momentarily towered over him before crashing over the side of the boat, swilling it clear. All he remembered seeing was his brother's angry face and dark eyes where passion and fury raged like the storm, then suddenly he felt his powerful hold on his arm.

'I said you'd be in the way!' Toni hissed as the rain and the wind lashed his dark hair into thongs whipping his face.

'It's my right...' gulped James.

'Over my dead body!' roared Toni just as the next wave thundered down on the little craft. He was powerless as the pitching hurled him across the deck.

'Man overboard!' cried Meredith. 'Get the life belt, Moby, James has gone overboard!'

The old deck hand clutched the railing as if he wanted to crush it.

'It's no use,' he said calmly. 'It's too late. It's no good...'

Meredith grabbed him by the scruff of the neck. 'You wouldn't be planning to let him drown maybe?' he snapped hotly and slapped him across the face. 'Pull yourself together, man. Toni'll get him out...'

'No!' cried moby, his hardened features crumbling to a grey morass. 'Not Toni as well! Oh God...' Then he pointed through the spray. 'The rocks ... We're on the rocks...' There was relief in his cry.

With the cracking sound of splintering wood the ship

31

suddenly pointed upwards like a finger accusing heaven.

'Hold on, Moby! We're very near the shore.' But even as he spoke he realised Moby would do very little to help himself.

'I've nothing more to lose,' he was complaining as Meredith struggled to get a hold on him.

'No time for soul-searching. Toni's a strong swimmer. They'll be all right, the beach is close . . .' He couldn't let the old man see his own fear. The sea was treacherous.

'I'm sorry, Meredith,' protested the old man, struggling to free himself. 'It looked such an easy way oot . . . I could nay help myself. I was afraid for Toni when James turned up. Ye see, Millie had told me ye'd adopted our child so she could come south to join me. . . It wasn't difficult to know Toni was mine, even after all these years. Ye always were so much harder on him . . .'

Meredith didn't answer, he needed his breath for the tremendous effort of reaching the beach with his senseless burden.

'I had such hopes of Toni inheriting,' Moby gasped, leaning against the reassuring firmness of the cliff which rose from the beach like a prison wall.

Meredith spat out a mouthful of sea water. His foam-laden beard hid his face. 'I was going to leave it to Toni, anyway,' he said, wringing out his handkerchief. 'Toni was my son, Moby. It's James we adopted when you and Millie left. If you hadn't been so busy enjoying the bright lights you would have known our first-born died . . . James inherited your love of the bright lights. Toni had a man-size job to do.'

'Oh God! You cannay let this happen to me!' murmured Moby, grasping the situation. 'Oh God, to think I was watching my own son drown . . .'

He watched Meredith remove his sea-logged boots. 'I

had nothing to leave him. Now there's nothing to inherit anyway!' He started to laugh uncontrollably. He moved slowly towards the thick white blanket of foam beyond which the waves still pounded the rocks.

'Hey! Where are you going? Come back, you old fool!' commanded Meredith as Moby broke into a trot.

Several seconds later when he reached the water's edge the strewn rocks stood like sentinels, around which even the swirling sea seemed to retreat defeated. For a moment he leaned on one of these staunch guardians of the sea's secrets, then raising his arms to heaven he yelled for all the crags to hear: 'Och man! How ambition blinds ye, and destroying the things ye love most ye then accuse God !'

The thick white foam lay like a shroud all around him, whilst the overpowering suction of the under-current sapped at his feet.

When the storm had abated, a seagull wheeled in the slate-grey sky where watery clouds were being teased out. The steady incoming waves breaking against the rocks was the only sound among the crags where deserted nests awaited the return of their occupants. She landed gracefully on the narrow strip of clean sandy beach, deserted but for two peaceful young men.

6

The Mountain Goat

The hills at the foot of the purple mountains rang with the song of birds and the fields seemed littered with dancing patterns of colour as Steven and Marion Trevellian chugged along the dusty ribbon lined with twisted olive trees. Their pre-war convertible pitched and rolled, leaving a curtain of dust to settle lazily, hiding their happy faces from the world. Their eyes screwed up against the sunlight, searching the face of the cliffs for a glimpse of the Italian cottage which was to be their honeymoon home.

'I never thought life could be so exciting!' exclaimed Marion. Her exuberance seemed to tingle to the very tips of her long slender fingers as her hands cupped her square face, keeping the loose strands of her long blonde hair out of her eyes. 'How different from stuffy old London!'

'I'm not at all sure you won't regret this.'

'Oh Steven! What a pessimist you are. I know my own mind.'

'But your father was right,' persisted Steven, frowning momentarily as his strong sun-burned hands tightened on the wheel and he negotiated the first tricky bend of their painfully slow ascent. 'A rich young debutante with London at her feet, cutting herself off from family, not to mention friends, fortune, civilisation, for an infatuation.'

'To become the wife of the world's future Great Master! Think of it, Steven, the biographies and novels about the life and love of Steven Trevellian ... And behind all great men' – she turned to face him and her grey eyes almost looked blue as they reflected the bright intensity of the sky – 'is a woman.'

'Women, my dear, in the plural.'

She studied his well-defined profile, and wondered how many fingers had traced his clean-cut jaw and his stubborn chin, and how many 'others' had kissed his smooth full lips.

'In the past tense,' she corrected him, clasping her hands in her lap, partly in self-defence as a twinge of conscience overcame her. What right had she, after all, to blame the girls who'd lain in his arms before she had met him, except that now she was his wife. 'It's the future I'm interested in,' she added with conviction, and stared straight ahead with over-emphasis.

Her words seemed to bounce back at her from the solid stone rocks which lined the narrow road, almost as if the mountain itself challenged her. She did not dare look at Steven again until they had emerged from the funnel and found themselves on a sunlit plateau where the lime-washed cottages clung to the sides of the mountain. Their cheerful walled gardens dripped into the olive groves like cream over a syrup pudding.

'It's not changed,' stated Steven as he stopped the engine and leaned on the driving wheel, staring through the vapour rising from the bonnet. 'Peaceful.'

He got out of the car, and without looking at her, reached the edge of the cliff in a couple of giant steps.

Marion watched him, undecided about whether to follow him or wait. A pang of jealousy gripped her as she

35

noticed the smile which creased his rugged weather-beaten face where the sunlight, reflected from the barren countryside, accentuated every ridge, deepened every grove, until his features resembled a mask in whose lines were sealed the memories of the past, a seemingly happy past. She felt she could compete with another woman but wondered, despondently, how one went about handling a mountain!

A few goats bounded into sight, bleating as if in welcome, and he waved. It was almost with relief that she heard the girlish voice which answered his greeting.

'I'd forgotten little girls grew up!' Steven said as the slender creature emerged from the cliff with the agility of her goats.

'It seems many years . . .' she laughed breathlessly, and the sun played gaily on her small white teeth, seemingly enjoying its own reflection in their pearly perfection.

'You've hardly changed, the same big watery eyes, the same agility . . . Only the hair . . .' He seemed to look too long and too searchingly into the small olive face for Marion's liking, and she felt it quite unnecessary for him to stroke the long raven plaits wound, like a crown, round the girl's head. 'Gone are the pigtails!' he added jokingly, and the girl threw back her head with swanlike grace emphasising the long curved neck.

'No more pulling, it used to hurt!' she teased laughingly.

In spite of herself Marion had to admit there was a certain charm in the Madonna face, unspoiled by make-up, as the long protective lashes fluttered a moment. She would be the envy of the best London models, she reflected.

'Come and meet my wife. Marion, this is Maria-Teresa. She was no more than a lanky teen-ager when I knew her during the war.'

He sounded a trifle too casual, thought Marion, as she watched the girl wipe her hands on her apron before extending one in greeting.

'I do hope you will be very happy here,' she said simply with a slight blush, then turning back to Steven she added quickly, 'Grandmother is preparing your favourite meal. I'll go and help her now.'

For a moment the face of the sun was smeared with a small white cloud which cast a deep shadow across his features, but Steven was still smiling as Maria-Teresa disappeared after her impatient goats, and for some reason, Marion felt relieved that he didn't gaze after her.

'When God comes to separating the sheep from the goats, he's going to have a hard time finding a place for her,' Steven mused, smiling once again as he reviewed some incident of the past without sharing it with her.

For a moment she hesitated, on the verge of voicing a sharp repartee, but the warmth of the sunshine and the lazy weight in her limbs helped her to acquire a certain magnanimity. After all, she thought reasonably, if the girl had meant anything to him, Steven would have married her, and had he meant anything to her, surely her soft musical voice would not have sounded so genuinely happy and unresentful on meeting his wife.

She put out her hand, invitingly, and Steven grabbed it hurriedly, smiling warmly into her grey eyes as he sat down beside her.

'Well, Mrs Trevellian, we are home at last. Just another few yards and you'll catch a glimpse of it ... Keep your eyes skinned.'

He didn't let go of her hand until they had reached the end of the track which led to the steps, steep steps winding upwards through wild flowers crowned by the soft yellow shower of mimosa cascading like a curtain half hiding the lime-washed cottage. But as it swayed Marion could see the open door, inviting, and enticing them to the cool shade of the sprawled vine untidily camouflaging the roofless porch. She caught her breath.

'It's far more beautiful than your picture!' she said in spite of herself.

In the soft light of the candle Maria-Teresa had placed on their supper table, Marian felt the overgrown vine assume new dimensions; she warmed to its mysterious hidden charms buried in the depths of its many shadows.

'How still it is in the mountains,' she whispered, not to break the spell, but a moment later Steven shattered the night air, sending the champagne cork to a hidden grave in the darkness.

'It'll get very cold.'

'The pessimist again! I would never have thought there could be such utter peace in our noisy world. It's like a small corner of Paradise dropped from heaven just for us. Oh Steven, I'm so happy!'

'I'm glad.'

But as he looked at her over the bubbling glass he held out, his eyes were far more eloquent and she felt like melting under his intense stare. The click, as their glasses met, was like the closing of a gate, locking them mysteriously in each other's orbit, completely unaware of Maria-Teresa's unobtrusive service as she brought her grandmother's special dish.

For a moment her serious olive features deepened with a guilty flush. Understanding a deeper meaning in the cryptic sentence, she had the feeling of having intruded upon a sacred moment. The hope in Steven's eyes, as if suddenly released from the bondage of doubt and the happiness which replaced it almost made her heart burst with pleasure. She quietly retreated.

'Hey, watch it!' scolded her grandmother as Maria-Teresa hugged her off her feet. 'What's made you so flushed and happy?'

'Love, grandmother, love. Isn't it wonderful when you see two people so deeply in love they forget the rest of the world around them. They're like rain drops running down a window pane, they run along side by side for a while, then suddenly rush into a head-on collision, and splash! They don't exist any more. They are transformed into something far greater than they were before, it shines in their eyes. They glow, like glow-worms in the night. I feel I can believe in transfiguration when I see people in love...'

'Just you get on with your work, my girl, and stop all this nonsense. If Father Peroni heard you he would give you an extra three Ave Marias for penance next Saturday.'

'What for?'

'Well, for allowing your imagination to run wild and interfere with your work. Not attending to your duties with dilligence ... Maria, why are you wrapping yourself in that shawl? Where are you going?'

'To the mountain, grandmother. So my heart can be stilled by its silence and peace, and I want the stars and the moon to know just how happy I am tonight.'

'No good will come of this running to the mountain business. You'd best help me clear up.' But as the old woman turned to glower at the table, it was already tidy. 'She's a good girl, really,' she smiled.

'The mountain air is doing you good,' said Maria-Teresa as she brought Marion some cold milk. 'You looked so tired when you first arrived. Now even your eyes look different, blue, like the sky. It's a happy colour.' She tidied up the magazines which had slipped off Marion's lap, then asked abruptly, 'Are you happy here?'

'Yes, of course.' For a moment Marion wanted to say more but she didn't know how to phrase her thoughts. She wanted to say 'Thanks for all your kindness, you and your grandmother have done so much for us ... But for all that, I'm getting rather bored.' Instead she remembered the first row she had with Steven when she'd plaintively complained she would like to look after him herself.

'You'd never cope with the stove!' he'd laughed rather cuttingly as a reminder that even in their London penthouse she'd never succeeded in making breakfast without burning the toast, over cooking the eggs, or letting the milk boil over.

'But this is supposed to be my home and it's the old woman who does all the cooking, and Maria-Teresa who does everything else ... including cleaning your brushes and tidying your studio. You never allow me near your work!'

'Only because you would distract me. Would you sooner I took more notice of her?'

But Marion was not at all reassured by his teasing. A smile puckered the corners of his eyes. They shone with an almost luminous green, she thought, enhancing his tan, and at any other time she would have loved to run her fingers through his tumbled fair hair.

'Sometimes I feel that you share a secret world with that little goat, and you won't let me into it. I'm rather bored with this pastoral scene and peasant life. How long before we go to Rome as you promised?'

'As soon as I have something to sell. Why don't you go? I'll be fine.'

Marion remembered the harsh things she said in her

40

hurt pride. Now she looked at the girl's innocent eyes and, on impulse, asked, 'Are you really happy here? Cut away from civilisation . . . with nothing for a young girl to do, nowhere to go . . . You could be a model!'

The olive face turned a deep pink and for a moment Marion felt uncomfortably aware of those large brown eyes, as if they had been able to read her most inner thoughts, and Maria-Teresa had understood her resentment.

'After all,' went on Marion, trying to justify herself, 'you are very beautiful, and why shouldn't you make a lot of money? It could help your grandmother too. You could buy her new gadgets . . . Make her life easier . . . I wouldn't hesitate if I had your looks.

'I love the mountains, and my goats. Where else could I be so happy? Money is all right, but here we don't really need so much of it. One day I might marry and I'd like to be here so I can bring up my children to love the mountain and learn its secrets.'

'Secrets?'

'The mountain often talks to me. I tell it all my thoughts, sad or happy, and it answers me in the songs of birds, the bleating of the goats the sigh of the wind . . . even the way the flowers dance and sway . . . It's a whole symphony. Only when it is completely silent am I frightened.'

'But it's always silent!'

'Peaceful, quiet, but never silent.'

Marion watched her disappear into the darkness of the doorway and smiled complacently. 'I would never have thought a little peasant girl with so little knowledge of the world could have such fanciful ideas!'

She had not realised she had spoken her thoughts aloud and was quite shocked when a shadow fell across her face and a smooth voice answered her.

41

'Perhaps it is because of her lack of knowledge of the world that she can be so happy and uninhibited.' Father Peroni smiled graciously as Marion made an effort to rise. 'Please don't disturb yourself, I've only come to pay a momentary call. I'll sit on this wall.' For a moment his gaze swept over the view of the mountain, then, as if there had not been a pause at all, he went on, 'At one time I was afraid that, coming into contact with someone as sophisticated as yourself, might bring a profound change in Maria-Teresa. It is only natural that people should talk, and compare their lot with yours ... and some feel that maybe the city has more to offer them.'

'But she would have a better chance of finding herself a husband!' The tone of her voice made the old man look intensely into her eyes and once again Marion felt uncomfortably aware of having laid her thoughts bare. She blushed, for the first time in her life, feeling conspicuous and unprotected among these mountain people.

'With her southern sultry looks she could even be spotted by some big film producer, or an artist in search of a model. After all, let's face it, there's nothing for a girl to do here. I'd be bored to distraction!' she added flippantly, to cover up her embarrassment.

'Maria-Teresa is in no need to seek a husband,' Father Peroni said quietly. His well-modulated voice retained a perfect calm which only added to Marion's discomfort. 'She has already dedicated her life.'

'A vocation? Do you mean she ...? Oh but that's monstrous! A nice girl like her...' Marion shrugged her shoulders to hide her shudder but Father Peroni left without enlightening her. His steady gaze held what looked to Marion like compassion, as if it were she who ought to be pitied.

* * *

'I am sorry,' apologised the old woman as she served dinner, 'but I don't know what has happened to Maria-Teresa. She left early this afternoon for the mountain...'

'She told me she often goes up,' interrupted Marion. 'She'll be all right.'

The old woman shook her head. 'I told her nothing good would come of this, it is too dangerous to come down those tracks in the dark. She will have to stay up there until morning.'

'What's all this about?' asked Steven as the old woman retreated. 'I've never known her not to return with her goats.'

'Oh, she's probably having a last fling. Father Peroni was telling me this afternoon that she's going to a convent. She's dedicated her life.

Steven turned white and, though she tried to draw him into conversation, he remained silent throughout the meal.

'No coffee for me,' he said, rising suddenly from the table. 'I think I'll get some fresh air before turning in. Don't wait up for me.'

Before she could protest, he was out of the cottage and the darkness of the mountain had effectively engulfed him.

It wasn't long before he reached the spring where he knew he would find her; the soft gurgle of the crystal water acted as background to her song as she bathed. Steven stood in the shadows, unable to break the spell by intruding, content to watch the silvery play of water over her softly rounded shoulders as if she were a Grecian statue in some famous garden.

'The moon is kind to illuminate such beauty with

such delicacy,' he said at last, stepping forward to catch her in his arms.

'Oh Steven, you should not have come!' But the sentence was denied by the warmth of her embrace. Half laughing, half crying, she scolded him, 'Now you are wet and will catch cold!' But his lips were on hers before she could say more.

As she lay, at peace in his arms, and the warmth of their bodies emphasised the scents of the wild herbs they lay in, Steven admitted, 'It was not until tonight that I realised just how much I have always loved you, and needed you ... Oh Maria-Teresa, I'm sorry for all the wasted years. I didn't think you would wait for me ... You know what it's like in war, one makes these wild promises ... But I think I always knew ... That's why I came back. I had to.'

'I always knew I loved you! But I thought you were happy with your wife. Until ... well, until those letters. When she found them she was so hurt I thought my heart would break.'

'You mean she was furious. You know she is leaving me?' he ignored her protests.

'She was hurt, almost humiliated ...'

'She could never live with a failure, all those letters turned me down. I'm no good as a painter...'

'Why not follow my advice? You paint so much better in words ... your poems are masterpieces; paintings. Something I could never hope to do as I never had the education, but you can put into words more than the brush can put on the canvas. You are not a failure, don't give up now. She'll be just as proud of you...'

'No, it's too late, and I am really rather glad in a way because I couldn't live with a lie... I love you, Maria-Teresa! As I never loved anyone else.'

He held her tight in his arms, caressing her gently as

she buried her face in his neck and whispered encouraging words in his ear. 'You are no failure ...' she reassured him.

There was no telling how long they lay there in each other's arms, but it was her acute hearing, accustomed to the mountains' echoes, which brought them back to reality.

'They have sent out a search party. Someone is in trouble...'

'They are probably searching for you, my silly little goat!'

'No, Steven, they would not send a search party for me. They would know where to find me and they are on a track no local would use. It is very dangerous, it must be a stranger...'

'God! It must be Marion, she must have gone in search of me...' He held her at arm's length, searching her face, 'Don't ever feel guilty about our love, it's about the purest thing which ever happened to me. Can you look at me straight in the eyes and say the same?'

For a moment they held each other's gaze, and there was no need for words.

It seemed she had been sitting on the ledge for ages after Steven left her, unable to bring herself to come down from the mountain. With her acute hearing she heard Steven's voice urging Marion to go back slowly, warning her the track was dangerous.

'One false move and you could cause a landslide...' Then a touch of anger sharpened his voice. 'What the devil were you doing?'

'Following you.'

'I told you I wanted some fresh air and not to wait for me.'

'That's what made me suspicious...'

'See what your suspicion's led to! Endangering the lives of half the villagers!'

It was then the crash happened. There was a scream, then everyone seemed to shout at once, orders and comments simultaneously, and the sounds became incoherent.

'Ah!' There you are,' stated her grandmother calmly as she entered the kitchen. 'I don't know where you've been, my girl, but I'd sooner not know. There's been enough trouble for one night ... Mr Steven had a bad accident trying to rescue his wife. I was glad you weren't here as I know how much they both mean to you. I think Father Peroni is driving them down to the hospital ... Come, child, you look all in ... I knew it would be a shock for you, but you'd learn about it sooner or later. Best come from me.'

The hot wine she sipped as she sat by the fire her grandmother had stoked up did little to revive her and she felt she would never again be wholly alive. Some part of her had died.

Even when Marion came back to the cottage later to pack her belongings, she couldn't bring herself to ask how Steven was.

'No. Leave those,' Marion said tersely, as Maria-Teresa started to add Steven's things to the cases. 'I don't know what he'll be doing when he comes out of hospital. Maybe he will come back here. I don't care, I'm through with him. Not even one painting accepted to make this nightmare worthwhile!'

For a moment she sobbed like a child and Maria-Teresa put her arms around her comfortingly. 'He hasn't failed you,' she tried to reassure her soothingly.

46

'Give him a little more time...' But even as she spoke she knew Marion's mind was made up.

'All the time in the world won't help him now. He's blind! You can burn those worthless canvases in your wretched stove ... He's blind!'

It was a beautiful spring day when the birds seem to sing louder and the flowers look more brilliant, and the light seems brighter. Even the rough track which twisted through the olive trees felt smoother, and the narrow road through the funnel less tortuous and menacing. Marion sat, silent and still next to her father, until they reached the sunlit plateau.

'It hasn't changed,' she said quietly, remembering with a pang that those had been Steven's very words the first time she'd emerged from that dark funnel two years ago.

'For the life of me I don't understand why you wish to come back! What a dump of a place ... It's very silence is depressing.'

'Maybe I was a little hasty in divorcing him. After all, now that he has become so famous I might persuade him to move back to civilisation.'

'Beats me what the critics see in his painting now which they missed two years ago. I suppose they have fads. Well, if we must go all the way, let's go and get it over with...'

The cottage door was locked, and the curtains at the windows drawn.

'That's unusual,' Marion told her farther. 'All the time I was here I never knew them to shut the door, let alone lock it!'

'Well, that simplifies things. Now we can leave with a clear conscience. After all, my dear, what could you possibly do for him, even if he changed his mind, or was in need of help, or what have you? Surely you wouldn't want to remarry the fellah!'

Marion wasn't listening to her father, she was groping her way through an outbuilding where every available space was occupied by canvases. She recognised a few, though they appeared altered, incredibly beautiful in fact. And every one signed by Steven Trevellian.

'But these dates don't coincide. It's before I left him, and he was not painting like this ... And these! These are recent ones. Look, father, this one is only half finished ... Do you think he has regained his sight?'

'Dashed good,' agreed her father. 'Almost better than his poems. Not that I approve of poetry, but he is doing very well out of it ...'

'I saw your car, I hope you don't mind if I take the liberty of enquiring what you want?'

Marion hadn't forgotten that well-modulated voice.

'Father Peroni! Perhaps you can tell me where Steven is. It seems to me that even though he is famous at last, he is in hiding ... And what happened to little Maria-Teresa, is she happy in her convent?'

'Convent?' The old priest's eyes widened, 'Maria-Teresa never went to a convent. She was a dedicated person ...'

'Yes, I remember you telling me ... She had a vocation, and ...'

'And you jumped to the conclusion that it was religious.' He shook his head wisely. 'No, she was dedicated to art. Ever since she was a little girl she painted on the walls of her cottage or drew in the dust of the road.'

'So this isn't Steven's work?'

'He must never know. She wanted him to write instead, and gradually sent out his canvases one by one as she finished them ... It gave him a new lease of life.

48

When he thought they were selling on their own merit he got down seriously to writing and has never looked back.'

'But why is the cottage locked up? Is it for privacy?'

Father Peroni turned his face towards the mountain and sighed.

'He wants to be alone. A wooden hut was all he wanted, up there, in the mountain, by the spring ... He loved her very much ...'

'Did he marry her?'

'Yes. Oh, I know what you are thinking. Was it moral as he was divorced? I used my own discretion. In my eyes he'd never been married. A registrar wedding only, a passing affair ... Also she was carrying his child by then. She'd faithfully waited for his return all those years; you see, they'd made their vows during the war when he was hiding here as an escaped prisoner. When you left him, there was no reason why they shouldn't marry.'

'Well, that's that,' stated her father emphatically. 'Now, if we hurry we can just be back in time for drinks.'

'Father!' cried Marian hotly. 'Do you ever think of anything but your comforts? I was married to him once ... And I think I still love him in a way, no matter what happened ...'

She felt herself blush for the second time in her life as Father Peroni gazed at her.

'Is the child like him?' she asked tentatively.

'Both child and Maria-Teresa ...'

'Oh no! Poor Steven!'

'During childbirth,' concluded the old man, warming to her sudden human interest and cry of the heart. Had she been able to read his mind she would have been gratified to know she had at last won his heart.

He stood silently by her side as she read the inscription on the grave: 'She lives for ever in the song of the

49

birds and the bleating of the goats, the scent of wild flowers and the breeze in the olive groves, my little mountain goat.' Steven's words were carved deeply and indelibly in the very rock of the mountain she had so loved.

Father Peroni guided her away from the cemetery. There was compassion in his eyes as he watched her take her place beside her father. The engine revved up unnecessarily loudly as the car pulled away creating a curtain of dust.

7

The Golden Christmas

As a teenager before the war, and before the rash of buildings, we lived in a large lonely house on the Belgian coast, surrounded only by sand dunes, and sea. The church was a good 20 minutes' walk across those dunes.

On Christmas Eve the main task was to decorate the tree and the house. Pictures were framed with holly and lampshades camouflaged with tinsel and crêpe paper. The dining table was extended to its full size and each place setting was individually decorated. All this is common-place in most households as the minutes tick away on the eve of the great day. However, one thing stands out in my memory which made this Christmas Eve different.

My special task had been to arrange the crib and the floral displays. By 11 o'clock we looked around us in wonder at the transformation. Everything was set for tommorow's feast. Then, well muffled against the cold night air, we each lit a fairylight fastened to the end of a long stick and started our trek across the sand dunes. As the numerous little groups neared the church, the countryside became a fascinating kaleidoscope of ever-changing patterns and colours. The night throbbed with song, and everything appeared to converge on the brightly lit church.

Inside, the place of honour, after the altar, was the Crib. In a living tableau set in a grotto, the school children represented the Holy family, the shepherds, the kings, and the angels. A large blue-eyed doll incongruously represented the infant Jesus. The flickering candles on the altar were reflected in the golden ornaments displayed among a profusion of flowers. The priests wore golden vestments, and the little choirboys looked uncomfortable in their red robes and starched lace ... we sang the well-loved '*Minuit Chrétiens*', 'Nöel' and 'Holy Night', feeling very much part of this Christmass, identifying ourselves with this simple family scene, and beyond it, in some uncanny way, shared the peace and goodwill far and wide with the rest of the world.

Good wishes were exchanged as the little groups relit their fairylights, and slowly the luminous kaleidoscope melted among the dunes and night returned to its former stillness.

Christmas Day was an hour old as we drank our hot soup. The tree was lit and we gathered round the crib for a final hymn before going to bed, dreaming of the rest of Christmas Day stretching out before us. But for me the true Christmas was over. It had been a golden moment at dead of night when a whole congregation had fused in mind and spirit, giving itself freely to make the Church of Christ alive; at one with all its living members, actively sharing the responsibility of its true meaning.

This was when we were children and before consumerism converted Christmas into Big Business. As we grew up and started to question and learn that this beautiful myth of our childhood was not the true story and, later still, when we were able to learn more about the

Nag Hammadi, and the Dead Sea Scrolls, our doubts and queries were answered. The truth was that the Gospels and Bible were the expurgated result of the Council of Nicea in 325 AD, as was the proclamation of Divinity (by vote) of a truly revolutionary man who never claimed to be more than heir to the throne: 'Christ' being the title of the heir to the throne of the house of David; like Dauphin in France or the Prince of Wales in the UK. This meant that the Church had all along taught, and demanded implicit faith, on false premises.

The man, Jesus, might well be accused these days of being a terrorist fighting against Rome, and even some of the hierarchy of Judaism. Indeed, Rome did consider him an enemy of the state as crucifixion was the penalty of such a crime, not for thieves or robbers. He survived, thanks to a potion (the sponge) and was cut down from the cross after only six hours, whereas it would take many hours, even days, for a healthy man to die. His eldest son inherited his title and position in 73 AD.

Would he not appeal far more to the younger generation as a 'freedom fighter' than the meek and mild lamb, which he was not, or, falsely, an elected divinity begotten by another personalised divinity full of the human faults of those who created him in their own image: 'vengeance is mine . . .'

Taken out of his historical setting he makes no sense. It is time for the Church to let him be known, and seen, in the context of his real role: the central figure of the politics of his time, leading a resistance movement, neither poor, nor born in a stable, but an aristocrat who urged his followers to arm themselves with the best swords they could afford (Luke). A man determined to fulfil the prophecies promised his people in their quest for a restoration. Surely it would not detract from, but add to the myth, especially his efforts to introduce democratic reforms to an elitist Cabalistic religion.

Christmas has nothing to do with his birth, which took place in March 7BC. But Christmas will, no doubt, keep its appeal as the 'season of good will'. It had, after all, been an ancient festivity long before the Church adopted the winter solstice into their calendar.

8

Abroad In Our Own City

Now that the children are back at school is the time for us to go to the library and find some historical facts and places about our own city. It is surprising what a wealth of history can be found sealed in some old building, gate, or street, bridging the gap of time.

It is more fun to choose a particular subject or period and try to find buildings and trades introduced in your city at that time. Then visit the buildings yourself, making notes of peculiarities, anecdotes and historical facts, as well as noting the route you took.

Next make a list of books on the costumes, habits and history of that period available at your local library.

Thus armed with all the material, organise a game for the holidays in the form of a treasure hunt, with the clues along the route you have carefully studied. When the children find the first building, gate, statue, or whatever it is, give as much detailed information about it as you were able to gather, before they go on to the next.

It is a good idea, if possible, to keep to one type, for example, all doorways, or all façades, or all statues. This tends to make a greater impression on the mind.

Follow these expeditions up with a supply of reading material on the chosen subject or period which the children can read in the evenings or on rainy days. The artistic ones might spend the rainy days painting repro-ductions of what they have seen.

Another fascinating pastime which can be associated with this treasure hunt of your city's past is terracotta modelling. Books on this subject can be found at your library in the children's section, even giving easy-to-follow instructions on how to build a little kiln in your back garden.

A useful substitute for those who are not sure they want to model enough to warrant building a kiln, is to put their objects under the grate in the fireplace, mak-ing sure to remind everyone *not* to rake the ashes! After a day or two the pieces are dry enough and can be taken out. The next step is to build a good fire in the grate and place the models in it for firing; once again make sure no one pokes the fire or the objects will be spoiled. Leave to cool and don't be too impatient to take things out before they are quite cold. These models can be decorated with oil paints.

Hours will be happily spent making models of tools, weapons, modes of transport and little figurines of the period of history you choose to study and all the best works could be given away as Christmas presents!

At the same time you will have brought 'living' history within the children's orbit, making it part of their field of vision and thought instead of it being a long list of names and dates. And you yourself may well be sur-prised at how little you really knew about your own town and its history. This idea can be applied to villages too. The vicar can usually help find history in the parish records.

A variation of this holiday game, providing you at least have bicycles, is to do what we did a few years ago. We decided on a 'King Alfred' holiday. After reading a few books, noting dates and places of battles and meetings, we went to visit all these places connected with King Alfred and his time. The holiday was a great success.

There isn't a corner of England which is not steeped in history. What better time than the hot dreamy summer days to make history come alive!

9

The Bidder

The particulars gave a glowing account of the country cottage with an acre of land: 'Ideal for the self-sufficient couple'. Ever since they had watched *The Good Life* on television, Mark and Jenny had dreamed of getting out of their rented rooms. Most of their friends had moved out into the country and they felt as if they had been left behind.

'The Hallidays,' Jenny sighed. 'They have that lovely old world cottage and Marjory is always complaining it is too small for her large parties. Just think of it, Mark!'

She pushed aside some of the children's toys and tried to make a semblance of tidying up the tiny living room.

'And John has to employ a gardener!'

'You sound resentful,' Mark scolded her.

'No, don't get me wrong . . .'

'I know.' He picked up the evening paper. 'I know the signs, you have seen an advert about a country cottage . . .'

'I've done better than that,' she retorted defiantly. 'I have arranged for us to get the keys tomorrow and we'll go and see it!'

* * *

The agent's office seemed quiet and harmless enough as Mark and Jenny first entered it, and his shrewd pale blue eyes danced with kindliness from the midst of the creases in his weatherbeaten face as he handed them the address.

'It's rather out of the way,' he started diffidently, 'but with a little enterprising effort and imagination it certainly has possibilities.'

'Has it been on the market long?' asked Mark.

'Oh, a few weeks...'

Mark looked up from reading the directions. The agent's evasiveness filled him with suspicions.

'Well,' went on the agent, 'six months to be exact...'

'I presume it is standing?'

'Structurally it is very sound but, well, you know what country places are like. A few alterations, and once there is water and electricity you could easily double its value.'

'I'm surprised some property shark hasn't snapped it up!' Mark stated, his enthusiasm for the place dwindling fast.

He was not very hopeful as he drove along the muddy track, which came to an end by a squeaking gate which limped sadly from rusty hinges.

The creeper-clad cottage seemed to sigh defeatedly as they opened its reluctant front door.

'Rather lonely, don't you think?' Mark suggested.

'Only because it's empty. Once it echoes with squabbling kids and is given a tonic of fresh paint and fresh air, it'll be very homely,' Jenny assured him.

'It smells damp...'

'Of course, but there are things one can do about that these days...'

She strolled dreamily round the overgrown garden. 'A few chickens, for eggs, a couple of ducks waddling across the lawn, a goat perhaps? Goat's milk is so good for children . . .'

He smiled as he watched her cheeks glow and her eyes shine with enthusiasm. She was right, of course, they'd lived long enough in small rented rooms where the neighbours complained constantly about the children's noise.

'Aren't you afraid we might lose all our friends?' Mark persisted. 'The agent was right, it is out of the way!'

Jenny was not to be put off. Her green eyes sparkled with determination and her husky voice held a note of conspiracy.

'Wait and see. By the time we've done a few repairs to it, given it a lick of new paint, it'll be the envy of them all.'

'But the woodwork wants renewing, and . . .'

'Even Marjory and John will be green with envy,' Jenny interrupted him. 'It'll be every bit as nice as theirs, one day!' She flattened the tip of his nose with her long supple finger. 'Wait and see!'

Mark knew better than to argue with her when she had made up her mind.

'All right,' he said on impulse, secretly pleased at the idea of John Halliday being envious. 'We'll tell the agent. I bet he'll be pleased to get this . . . thing . . . off his hands! It's not every day he meets a couple of escaped lunatics.'

He lost no time that evening in slipping round to their local pub to meet John and give him a glowing account of their find.

'It was so lovely there we stayed on a bit. Unfortunately, the agent's office was already closed when we

60

got back, but we'll be round first thing in the morning.' He grinned as he noticed he had John's full attention. 'So I'll be a little late getting into work tomorrow morning, if that's all right with you?'

John and he had worked together in the same office for years, but lately he'd grown tired of John's boasting about all the wonderful amenities they were enjoying, barely concealing his pity, just short of contempt, for their circumstances. 'Marjory,' John would say almost patronisingly, 'always admires Jenny, such a plucky little woman, so resourceful too. How she copes never ceases to amaze us! Of course we've grown so accustomed to having everything I'm sure we wouldn't know where to start if we were in Jenny's shoes. You're a lucky fellow, Mark...'

Damn the Hallidays! thought Mark as they re-entered the agent's office the following morning. Well, we'll show them! But his thoughts were jarred as he became aware of Jenny's husky voice.

'But that's much more than we offered on the phone last night, and you told us our offer was acceptable...'

'Yes, I'm sorry. It's quite amazing but several offers have come in.'

The agent's blue eyes looked coldly at her, half shaded by his knit brow. He waved a few papers, seemingly wanting to terminate the interview.

'But weren't we *first*?' Jenny challenged, feeling the room closing in on her and becoming clammy with the tense atmosphere of a court room awaiting the verdict of some invisible jury.

'The point is we must sell to the highest bidder. That's the law.'

The statement was so matter-of-fact she couldn't argue with it, but tossed her dark head angrily, battle shining in her eyes.

'We'll raise our offer then,' she snapped impulsively.

The agent's eyes brightened once more as he returned the papers on his desk. 'Of course you must understand my position,' he said calmly. 'I will have to advise the other party. I'll ring them straight away.'

'I'll wait,' stated Jenny, seating herself purposefully.

'Do you want it *that* badly?' asked Mark. But the answer lay in her eyes as she stared back at him with the despair of a cornered wild animal.

'I'm afraid my client wants the cottage in a hurry, her son is getting married and it is to be a wedding present...' The agent turned to the telephone, and when the ringing tone stopped Jenny involuntarily listened to the murmuring voice. It was blurred, but recognisable.

'Yes, Mrs Halliday, you want me to let your house ... Yes, I have customers interested. I think we can safely say there won't be any further offers to top yours ... The cottage is yours. I'll have the papers ready for you to sign by lunchtime.'

'Halliday!' cried Jenny aghast. 'She wants the cottage for her son? But he is only five years old!'

'Whatever his age it is immaterial to me. The fact is that she offered me twice as much as you have, and the law...'

'Requires you to sell to the highest bidder!' snapped Jenny curtly.

'For heaven's sake let her stick with it!' pleaded Mark, afraid Jenny would try to outbid the Hallidays. 'What can she do with it? She can't live in two cottages at once!'

They left the agent's office despondent.

'In all the excitement I forgot to tell you, John's been promoted to head office.'

'To London?' queried Jenny, disbelief ringing in her exasperated voice.

'Yes,' replied Mark calmly, 'so both cottages will be on

the market soon and you can have your pick!' He gave her a side glance but he knew what her answer would be. Neither of them would consider having anything to do with the Hallidays.

They didn't have to wait long. First thing the following morning the agent rang them up.

'Thought you'd like to know the Hallidays have backed out from the sale of the old cottage. They visited it last evening and were shocked by its condition.' There was a brief pause. 'So, if you care to come to my office about noon to sign the contract the cottage is all yours.'

As they were leaving his office after signing, the agent smiled at an elated Jenny and almost crushed Mark's hand in a tight grip. 'You need to be more careful in your choice of friends in the future,' he offered as his parting advice, his blue eyes twinkling mischievously.

10

Love Came in a Storm

Elisabeth's Mini-Cooper raced through the country lanes, her headlights cutting two distinct chunks out of the darkness of the night. With one hand she wiped away the tears which clouded her eyes, then suddenly, through the blur, two tiny specks of light stared straight at her, as if challenging her. Automatically she slammed on the brakes and her Mini jolted to a halt with a screech. For a second she saw what looked like contempt in those eyes, then, at the last minute the black cat streaked across the lane and disappeared into the hedge.

'That could bring me good luck!' she commented dryly, then shrugged her shoulders at the sound of her own voice.

She pulled into an open gateway, her hands still shaking as she rested them on the driving wheel. In her headlights she watched the lambs nestling by their ewes and a few cows lying close by the hedge stared back at her complacently. But once her headlights went out the countryside reverted to its peaceful night-time darkness and only the song of a distant nightingale could be heard, occasionally interrupted by the screech of an owl, forecasting doom to some small creature.

'Doom,' she said aloud, 'and no traces left! How

many of us will see the daylight?' She dug her hands deep into her pocket and fingered the small box. 'Not just yet ... I will have a cigarette and enjoy for a moment longer the peace and quiet the world only seems to offer those in harmony with nature.'

She wasn't quite sure how long she had sat there when she noticed the sky seemed darker; the clouds gathered on the thinly luminous skyline were rolling in towards her in the oppressive quietness. A few moments later it became obvious, even to Elisabeth, that she was in for a thunderstorm. Within minutes of the rain the red earth had turned into a sea of mud, the brambles sagged under the weight of the water, and the sheet lightning lit up a dismal scene in which she noticed, with horror, the brook had overflowed.

It was no use, the more she revved up, the more her wheels sank in the mud. She gave up at last, with a sigh of exasperation. The cows, lambs and ewes had disappeared. She was alone, curtained off from the world by sheets of rain. 'Well, wasn't that what I wanted?' she asked herself as the water from the brook swirled around her as if intent on swallowing her, Mini-Cooper and all, and washing away the traces of her brief existence. 'But not like this. I had it all so well planned until that damned cat crossed my path...' Once more she fingered the little box of sleeping pills. 'I wanted to fall asleep at the wheel. It would have looked like an accident and Harry need never have known...' But at the back of her mind the niggling truth prodded her conscience. 'Of course I wanted him to feel guilty! And why not, after he deceived me!'

She combed her fingers through her dishevelled hair and remembered how he used to curl the loose strands round his fingers and dreamily tell her it looked like liquid gold. Unconsciously she wrapped herself tighter in her coat and smiled as she felt the comfort of its warmth. Harry used to say the nicest things, making a girl feel wonderful...

From the very first, when she'd gone to that Boxing Day dance, alone because her sister had flu, and Tom, her current boy-friend, had refused to take her, preferring to go to the football match with his pals... Stiff and unsmiling, feeling conspicuously like a wallflower, she stood by the door, hoping he might have a change of heart – until a suave voice whispered: 'You shouldn't have come off the Christmas tree...'

She couldn't turn her head as a hand held her hair; the touch made her tingle gently, bringing a slow blush to her cold features.

'I still believe in fairies. Don't you?'

'Then it's time you grew up!' she retorted, smartly, she hoped.

'I'm glad I haven't, or I might have missed you ... Come, let's dance.' He turned her into his arms and smiled warmly into her large dark eyes. 'Now, now...' He stopped her protests. 'Just grant me this one wish before you disappear like Cinderella, or return to your tree-top.'

He was a beautiful dancer and it was the easiest thing in the world to follow him and relax in his arms. They waltzed under the mistletoe, and the melting process which had begun when he'd smiled at her was completed. She knew it was Christmas and that people did crazy things at parties, but this, she thought, was the *real* thing.

Throughout the winter they went out together and it became common knowledge that she and Harry were 'going steady'. She waited eagerly for the moment when he would make some suggestion about their future. Spring came, and summer waned into a golden autumn, and at last the great moment came.

'Liz,' he started awkwardly, 'you know there is nothing in the world I'd like better than . . .' He stopped as his fingers curled a loose strand of her hair. 'It's just like gold . . .' And he kissed her.

It was a while later before he returned to the subject. It was easier for both of them as he held her so closely their heartbeats almost sounded like one, and they couldn't see each other's eyes. His face buried in her long golden hair, he whispered, 'There's nothing in the world I'd like better than to marry you, Liz . . .'

It was a precious moment she would lock up for ever in her heart.

It was at the following Christmas party, as they danced under the mistletoe that she dared, at last, to question him more purposefully about their future.

'Why not announce our engagement now, Harry? It would be a fitting moment; it was at a Christmas party we met . . .'

'Well,' he hesitated, 'you can do. If you like . . . But . . .'

'But what, Harry? You haven't changed your mind about me, have you?'

'Heavens no! It's just that well, I'd like it to be our own secret.' He saw the question forming in her mind and anticipated it. 'I have a few things I want to put in order first. Then as soon as I get my promotion, we can leave together. It would give us a better start . . .'

It made good sense to her, at the time. Now she sat in her soaking Mini surrounded by flood water and wondered why she hadn't seen through him. She was cold, and she had smoked her last cigarette. Once again she fingered the little box, vaguely thinking it might be a suitable moment to draw the final curtain and skip the last act. She shuddered; it was too painful to bear, she knew she couldn't live with the memory of her child's face peeping out of the shawl as they took him away from her to await adoption. *This* was the moment, she decided, taking the box out of her pocket at last.

It was then she heard the roar of an engine between two claps of thunder; someone was shouting and cursing, a large hand banged at the window. When she looked up she could see nothing through the curtain of rain which spilled from the rim of his sou'wester, only the feel of his gaze and the light in his eyes.

'What the devil do you think you're doing sitting here?' he demanded curtly. The rain collected on the tip of his nose before pouring off it like an opened tap. He opened the door and grabbed her unceremoniously. 'Come on. I've got better things to do ... What idiotic shoes!' he exclaimed, surly, as he gathered her in his oilskin-clad arms as if she were a handful of weeds to be disposed of.

A few moments later she was uncomfortably jogging along rough tracks in a draughty Land Rover.

'What were you up to then? Alone in a country lane at night ... boyfriend let you down?' He seemed to sneer at her but his shrewd eyes glanced at the little box she still held in her hand. He swung the Land Rover through narrow gates and one of his large rough hands grabbed hers as they suddenly lurched. 'Hold tight or you'll be flung out ... Here, give me that box before you drop it and litter the countryside...' He took no notice of her protests and pulled up with a jerk in front of a stone-built farmhouse. He eyed her thin legs, knocking at the knees, and his lips curled, contemptuously, she thought. 'I reckon we could just fit you up with some of mother's clothes.'

He laughed goodnaturedly as he carried her over the threshold.

'The brides who crossed this threshold had to be made of better substance to survive ... A puff of wind would blow you away like chaff,' he added, with a pretence of throwing her up in the air. 'Hey, mother?' he called out as he dropped Elisabeth on the hearth by a large log fire, 'Got something a girl could wear?'

He threw her a towel and ordered, 'Hurry and get out of those wet things.'

A moment later a pink, plump, grey-haired little lady arrived, her rounded arms cradling warm-smelling flannels, a scent which took Elisabeth back to her childhood, when her mother would air her clothes in front of a fire.

'Let me help you, you poor little thing...' The grey eyes creased into a kindly smile and the round, red cheeks looked temptingly like peaches, soft and velvety. 'I've got some hot chocolate, that'll warm you up.'

Elisabeth was about to protest chocolate was fattening, and anyway she preferred black coffee; but the older woman was cocooning her in an over-large flannel dress as she added, 'I've had cocoa on all night with their comings and goings ... We've lost some sheep in this storm and Dick brought in the lambs...'

'And now I bring you the biggest sheep of them all!' he teased, leaning in the doorway watching them. There was a twinkle in his eyes as he noticed Elisabeth's confusion. 'Cocoa'll do you good, put a bit of colour in those pale cheeks.' He passed her a large mugful. 'Hurry up with it, there's work to do. What's your name?'

'Elisabeth,' she stammered. 'And I know nothing about farming.'

'You will by morning!'

She stared darkly at him, thinking his large frame filled the doorway as he stood there for a moment looking down at her, a small lamb in one hand and a black one under his arm. A couple of steps later he placed them on the rug at her feet. For a moment they wobbled, incapable of steadying their legs. The little black one bleated in distress. Elisabeth rushed to his help.

'How can you laugh at his misfortune?' she demanded accusingly as Dick chuckled. 'There,' she coaxed soothingly, hugging the lamb. 'What a horrid cruel world it is . . .'

'Nothing wrong with the world, it's the people in it . . .' Dick chided, holding out a bottle of warm milk. 'When you've fed those two there's another job for you.'

Elisabeth was about to state categorically that she wasn't a farm hand, but Dick didn't give her the opportunity. He looked at her with a mixture of severity and understanding. 'In the cowshed,' he added, in a tone which allowed no room for argument. Then he turned and left.

'I'll go, just you stay here and keep warm,' his mother suggested kindly.

'It's all right,' said Elisabeth quickly, realising the older woman had guessed her resentment at being made to work. Suddenly she was afraid she would appear ungrateful and for some inexplicable reason she found herself wanting Dick's mother to have a good opinion of her. 'Thanks, I'll cope.' she managed to smile. 'Just tell me where to go.'

'Playing nursemaid to a cow!' she said angrily, choking back the tears as she stood looking down at the huge brown mass. 'What does he take me for? He is a brute . . . Why did he have to barge into my life?'

The cow heaved and Elisabeth went week at the knees, wanting to run to the door, but unable to move with fright. The big brown head turned and the soft brown eyes stared at her sadly, seemingly recognising her inefficiency. The thunder was loud, too loud for Elisabeth's liking, and she realised the cow was as nervous as she was, especially now that the moment had come and the birth was imminent.

She fingered the little fringe between the velvety ears.

'All right, old girl, I know all about it. Only you're lucky. You'll be able to keep *your* baby ... But what was a girl to do when she finds out the father of her baby is already married?'

The cow looked at her as if she were weighing her up, wondering what sort of stuff humans were made of, and before Elisabeth realised what was happening the small wet calf was struggling in the deep bed of straw. Too busy licking her offspring, the cow never gave her another look.

'A hot bran mash,' Dick ordered as he checked the cow and calf. And when she returned with the bucket, he added, 'Fill up her hayrack with the best hay, from over there...' He tossed his head in the direction of a bale.

Daylight was coming through the wet panes of glass and Dick started the milking. 'Take some and feed it to those lambs,' he told her.

'What does he take me for?' she complained as she ran to the house through the pouring rain. She felt at a disadvantage, and to add to her discomfiture she realised it was the first time in her life she had been ordered about. 'Not even a please or thank you! Who the hell does he think he is!' She spat back at the rain which dripped from the tip of her nose.

* * *

71

But as she sat by the fire feeding the lambs, a content-
ment she'd never experienced before filled the hollow
she'd known until then.

'Nature is a wonderful thing,' said Dick's mother
quietly as Elisabeth stared at the basket full of eggs she'd
just brought in. 'Animals aren's as possessive as humans.
They give, whereas we take ... Most people only think of
what they can get out of life instead of what they can put
into it. I'm sure that's the wrong attitude. We could
learn a lot from nature you know.'

Yes, thought Elisabeth, feeling incredibly drowsy. She
was vaguely aware of the breakfast preparations going
on. But what can I give? Cows give milk; sheep, wool;
hens, eggs ... But me ...? She fell asleep.

She wasn't sure if it was a clap of thunder or the crash of
cutlery which woke her up.

'Heavens! Where am I?' she asked as Dick smiled
down at her, tray in hand.

'In bed. You fell asleep at breakfast time ...'

She sat up and stared at the great oak beams, the polished floor with its sheepskin rugs, and out through the
chintz-draped window. The sun lay low and pale
between the rows of willows edging the lane.

'Tea time?' she asked guiltily as Dick placed the tea-
tray beside her. 'But the lambs, who's feeding them?
Your mother's so busy.'

'She's quite used to coping.'

'But she could do with some help.'

'I reckon she could, but you know what they say about
two women in the same kitchen! Certainly she and my
wife never got on ...'

Elisabeth thought she could detect a note of sadness
in his voice but she was more preoccupied with her own

pain. 'I should have known! There always is a wife in the background!'

She was feeding the lambs when the police car arrived. At first the babble of voices didn't seem to concern her, until they came into the kitchen.

'They're making routine checks on a car,' said Dick. 'But as you see, officer, it's quite all right; she's staying here as general help around the farm. In fact,' he joked, giving her the faintest wink reassuringly as he could see her hands shaking, 'we think she'll make a pretty fair farmer!'

'That's all right, sir, but we must make these routine enquiries, especially when the family reports a missing person ... Leave it with me.' He smiled broadly, 'I'm sure you're right, you seem to have a good helper...'

'Now, young Liz,' started Dick after the police officer had left, 'I think you owe us some explanation.'

He lit his pipe and the smoke swirled, hiding his face, but Elisabeth felt very vulnerable under his invisible stare.

'You abandon your car on my land ...'

'You dragged me out of it!' she exploded defensively.

'But you are on my land, in my house, in fact...'

'You brought me here!'

'And your family don't know where you are ...'

'I'm over twenty-one.'

Dick took the small box of sleeping pills from his pocket and slowly, deliberately, placed it on the mantelshelf. His gaze was enough for Elisabeth to realise he had more insight than she had credited him with.

'Oh you, you brute!' she suddenly wept.

73

'I'm sorry if I haven't got genteel manners. I'll come straight to the point. Life is simple, and the world is all right. It's the people who complicate things. People create problems, they have to learn to live with them. I'm going out now to have a look at that cow.'

'How is the calf?' she asked despite herself.

'Dead.'

She buried her face in her hands and renewed her sobbing.

'She can have another calf later on, it's not the end of the world, Liz. Animals are more philosophical than we are. The important thing is for life to go on. Continuity...' he added as he reached the door.

'How easy it is for you to be smug about it when you have never suffered a loss!' she cried, full of self-pity; could she ever forget her pain?

She stared resentfully at him as he remained silent for a moment before closing the door.

'Don't upset yourself so.' His mother's gentle touch was surprisingly soothing and comforting as she put her arm around Elisabeth's shoulders.

She wasn't sure what it was about the older woman which made her open out, but she found herself pouring out all her problems in an almost incoherent torrent. There was neither surprise nor shock in Dick's mother's eyes as she smiled.

'Why don't we go to the home and collect your baby?' she said casually as if it were a daily occurrence. 'It's a good life on the farm...'

'But what about Dick's wife?'

Dick's mother paled visibly. 'She left ages ago...'

'Poor Dick!' Elisabeth murmured. 'Did he divorce her?'

'No. He loved her, understood her longing for the comforts of town and was certain she'd return when she'd had the baby . . . But she was too proud . . . took an overdose of sleeping pills . . .'

'And the baby?'

'Just before the birth. It was tragic.'

'It was criminal and selfish!' cried Elisabeth spontaneously. She ran to the comforting arms where she felt secure, and thought, At least I didn't kill my baby! But aloud she said, 'To think I called him a brute because I thought he had never suffered! I was so wrapped up in my own misery. I thought love was being cherished and spoiled by someone wanting to please you and make you feel special . . . Nothing to do with concern for other people's feelings. But it's like the storm, there, all around us, involving everything and everyone.' She stopped her outburst and asked, 'What about Dick? What would he think?'

'It was his idea, he heard you talking to the cow . . .' She smiled warmly as she watched Elizabeth's incomprehension. 'You don't think he left you all alone in the cowshed, do you? He was worried about what you might do next. Now, come along, let's not waste any more time, my dear . . .'

On the way to the home, Elisabeth was preparing herself for a complicated interview only to find that Dick had already rung up and paved the way.

'He's a lovely little fellow,' said Dick's mother, nursing the baby as Elisabeth drove back to the farm through the dark country lanes.

Suddenly two specks of light stared at her and she applied the brakes gently not to jog her passengers. 'A black cat has crossed our path!' she laughed. 'That should bring good luck . . .' Her headlights picked out the tyre marks she had engraved in the tarmac the night before.

The farmhouse door stood open, a cradle stood on the hearth rug where Dick had unceremoniously dumped her, but he stood smiling welcomingly as his mother placed the baby in the cot.

'Welcome home,' he offered her lamely. But the happiness which shone in his eyes filled Elisabeth with a new warmth and vitality. She rushed spontaneously to his arms, tears of joy running down her fresh pink cheeks.

Neither of them heard the footsteps in the hall. 'Excuse me,' interrupted the police officer, 'I found this little black kitten in the lane. Is it yours or shall I send it to the RSPCA?'

'Oh no!' cried Elisabeth. 'We'll take care of it ... Won't we?' She looked up at Dick enquiringly and was instantly struck by his strong masculine features. A real man, she thought, strong and understanding...

'Anything you say, my dear,' he said softly. Then turning to the mantelshelf, he reached leisurely for the small box, and handing it to the constable added casually: 'By the way, I found this in the lane. Some "towny" must have dropped it accidentally. No one around here needs these!'

11

The Laundrette Blues

'Why don't you stay in bed and get over this wretched cold?' asked James, looking critically at his wife's red nose and flushed cheeks. 'It's inconsiderate to spread your germs, and I have responsibilities at the office.'

'But there's all the washing!' Ursula protested between sneezes. 'If you weren't so stubborn we'd have a washing machine and I ... I...' She exploded into a sneezing fit.

James went to the door and eyed the overflowing linen basket just inside the bathroom. Normally he would have told her the washing should be done before seemingly all their dirty linen was in the basket. But, piqued by her accusation, he suddenly felt magnanimous.

'I'll take it to the laundrette myself,' he said, ignoring Ursula's sceptical glance.

It wasn't until he was struggling through the streets with his cumbersome load that he felt conspicuous. Most unbecoming, he thought, but a washing machine indeed! Women haven't enough to do; if they kept themselves occupied instead of reading magazines full of advertisements filling their heads with nonsense...'

He read the instructions carefully and followed them

scrupulously, then he got stuck, having forgotten the powder! He stared around for an assistant, but there was only a young man sitting, fidgeting as he stared out expectantly at the street beyond the glass door.

It required a tremendous effort for James to ask him, and the young man smiled, a little impatiently, thought James, as he showed him the machine on the wall.

'Put the little blue cup underneath, place your coin in the slot, and bob's your uncle. They think of every-thing...' He laughed, 'Mind you, you'd be surprised at the number of people who put their money in the wrong slots. That happened to me once!'

His clear unselfconscious laughter irritated James, who couldn't imagine anyone enjoying being laughed at.

'That, I may add, was my luckiest mistake. It started a beautiful romance!'

'Hardly a suitable place for a courtship,' remarked James, with appropriate disapproval ringing in his voice. 'A little too public, I'd say.'

It seemed to James that the large clear blue eyes which mocked him silently were making a critical survey of his well-tailored suit. He shrugged his broad shoul-ders and lowered his gaze sweepingly to the blue jeans and casual suede shoes and back again to the blond head with its cascade of unruly locks tumbling over a square forehead.

'Guess it's your first trip to one of these places.' The young man's powerful voice activated his Adam's apple, increasing the ivory gap above the polo-neck sweater and the chiselled jaw. 'Well, let me tell you, times have changed. Gone are the days when one washed one's dirty linen in private! The laundrette and the washing machine have come to stay. A permanent, solid feature of our modern world.'

'There was something permanent and solid about love in those days,' began James involuntarily. 'Now young people are in and out of love daily.'

Once again the young man's laughter irritated him; it was so obviously mocking him, and the standards he upheld. They have no morals, he reflected.

'Well, my fair damsel in distress lasted longer than that! You never saw such eyes ... Dark hazel, no, black, no ... They changed according to her mood from soft golden honey, to purple in sadness, or intensely dark with a touch of red, like burning coals in anger...' He walked leisurely over to the coffee machine. 'Tea or coffee?' he asked casually, before adding, 'You might think she had raven hair, but her oval face was framed with soft honey curls.' He turned and stared at James, coin in hand.

'Er ... tea, please,' James stuttered.

He took the carton absentmindedly, and grimaced as he discovered it was hot.

Ursula would have warned him! Ursula? There was a time when he might have described her much as this young man described his 'damsel', never to a stranger, though!

'She'd finished her wash,' went on the young man, cupping his hands round the carton of coffee for warmth.

Large hands, thought James, strong but not well cared for; they had cuts and stains. Unconsciously he looked down at his own well-manicured hands.

'I was just starting mine as she went to fetch a basket. I placed my coin in the slot and rammed it well in, then I sat down ... you should have seen her face when she opened the lid of her machine and got a splash of cold water instead of finding her wash spun dry!'

James smiled as he pictured Ursula in the same predicament. Cheeks red, the little vein in her neck swollen and throbbing, and her eyes would burn like smouldering coals. He looked at the young man. Strange that he should have described Ursula's eyes so accurately...

'Rather embarrassing for you,' he offered sympathetically.

'Embarrassing! She gave me a lecture rather like a Victorian maiden aunt rebuking an unruly nephew. *You* know the sort of thing.'

James flushed, did he think him *that* old-fashioned?

'But when she'd finished I bought her a cup of coffee and we became very good friends. Underneath that façade she was a very nice, lively person, poor thing...'

The sadness in the last remark made James look up. 'Why, what happened to her?' he asked, surprised to hear his own voice questioning someone else's affairs. 'Did she have an accident?'

'Nothing like that,' reassured the young man. 'No, I just feel sorry that such a beautiful creature should be married to such a mean old devil.'

'You knew her husband and yet you encouraged her?' James voice rang full of selfrighteous indignation.

'No,' interrupted the young man, who went on sarcastically, 'and she seldom talked about him. But as an artist I study people and put into my drawings what I see in them. I could see her suffering, trying so hard to be what he expected of her. No one has the right to dominate another's life. She was high-spirited, sensitive, artistic ... But tied to the kitchen sink by a Victorian husband who disapproved of gadgets. No tinned foods, packet soups, or modern aids generally.'

James undid his tie. 'Must be the heat ...' he stammered apologetically, realising he'd never done such a thing in his life. But the heat suddenly seemed suffocating and the machines louder.

Could it be Ursula? he wondered unhappily. But surely she knew he only cared for her wellbeing, moral as well as physical.

He watched the young man empty his tub and for the first time wondered if he *was* a little old-fashioned. He had been perfectly content with the quiet, well-regulated life Ursula had never openly objected to. Though on recollection she had sometimes listened to her friends' exploits with almost unbecoming longing.

'Well, that's my lot for this week,' smiled the young man. 'Hope you have better luck. Married women have a horrible habit of being faithful, and Jenny was no exception … My romance came to an end last week when her husband suddenly bought her a washing machine.'

James could hardly wait to get home. In 12 years he'd never felt such an urge to be close to his wife. On the way he stopped at the Electricity Centre. Flushed with a new sense of expectation, he took the steps two by two, almost rushing into the bedroom to spread the glossy pictures of washing machines on her bed.

'We'll go and choose one together as soon as you're well,' he smiled, and ignoring her red nose, he kissed her, seeing only the golden honey of her eyes.

12

The Evening Meal

Along the green sea stretches a long ribbon of golden sand softly undulating inland among the greeny motley of dunes. The red-tiled roof of a cottage slopes as low as the dunes themselves, turning its back to the sea, which provides its inhabitants with their livelihood, always meagre, often bitter, and marked by the fatal toll among the rugged menfolk. Yet, on the other side of the low-roofed cottage stands the cheerful lime-washed face of a welcoming home. The door stands half open, flanked on either side by green-shuttered windows. Red geraniums shiver in the breeze as they stand in rows, dramatically vivid against the tarred lower border of the wall. The path leading to the door is constantly swept to keep it free from the encroaching sands.

An old man in a red sail-cloth shirt straddles a chair, warming himself in the fickle sun. His hands shake as he holds them clasped over the back of the chair and his head nods from side to side. His eyes are mere slits in a wrinkled weatherbeaten face, their colour hidden by the shade of his bushy eyebrows, but their gaze is steady as he watches the progress of a black-shawled head bobbing through the dunes.

The old peasant woman opens the gate and struggles up the path, carrying a large bundle of dirty washing.

'*Avond.*' She nods her head in greeting.

The old man slowly removes the round clay pipe from his mouth. ''*Tis stiff coulden away,*' he answers – It's cold.

'*Niet in t'zon,*' she says – Not in the sun – as she heads for the outbuilding to deposit her burden, then, nipping off the faded head as she passed the geraniums, makes her way to the stable door of her kitchen.

It gleams with scrubbed floors and whitewashed walls adorned only by a couple of family photographs on either side of a large crucifix. On the mantelpiece stands a large inverted glass dome protecting the gaudy statue of a saint, at whose feet lies a wax rose. The long low range projects its bulbous hearth to the centre of the low-ceilinged room. She opens it to check the fire, then turns to place the enamelled coffee pot on the hotplate. The scrubbed wooden table and three chairs make up the furniture of the room. She spreads a red and white gingham cloth and from the recessed cupboard takes a pitcher of milk, a stone jar of butter, a crusty loaf, a couple of knives and two stone mugs. Her preparations completed, she turns to her black bag and takes out a large slice of cheese, bought earlier at the market, and adds it as a treat to their frugal evening meal.

Now she stands by the stable door and surveys her husband. Wrapped in a large black overall, her arms folded across her chest, she is ageless, timeless and raceless. Her clogs and speech alone are Flemish. Her sparse grey hair is pulled in a tight knot at the back of her head, her deeply wrinkled skin, burned by salt and wind, stretches over her cheekbones. Her eyes, grown small with age, appear to break into numerous slits at their corners; grooves, token of years of squinting into the biting salt-laden winds as she watched the sea, waiting for the safe return of the fishing boats. Her lips are thin and dry, and the clean-cut jawline is well defined and stubborn. Her neck is thin and stringy but she holds her head high and with great dignity.

With almost bovine placidity she accepts with resignation whatever fate brings her way. Her primitive instincts are touched with superstition but this does not debar her from the great inheritance she shares with her millions of sisters throughout the world; the Dignity of Man. They are welded together and merge over the centuries as a unified race.

It's no coincidence that the peasant of Flanders murmurs a silent prayer as she passes the wooden cross at the corner of the road, whilst her Tibetan sisters murmur '*Om Mani Padme Um,*' as they pass to the left of a Chorten. The Flemish woman kneels in prayer at the foot of a small statue of the Virgin tucked into a niche in a tree trunk, as her Himalayan sister adds a stone to the cairn at the top of a mountain pass. The one will cross herself, the other turn a prayer wheel, but to each it is an act as simple and necessary as breathing. The countless prayer flags fluttering from temples, houses and poles in Asia, or the little stone chapels, inconspicuous in the middle of Flanders' cornfields, are a concrete proof that there is no place remote enough to be separated from the universal consciousness which permeates creation and creatures alike.

It is no coincidence that the Norwegian peasant shares with her Nepalese sister a liking for brightly striped aprons. The former wearing hers in front as she stands at her sink, the latter behind as she sits to her work. Nor is it coincidence that inhabitants from Norway to the Alps and all the great range of mountains which sprawl across Europe and the Middle East, right down to the majestic Himalayas, use words easily recognised by most. It is simply proof of the kinsmanship which unites the whole of mankind.

The shade of their skin may vary, but the roughening of their hands by hard manual labour is the same. Their way of life neither requires nor demands much. They only want progress for their children, content to admire their advancement without envying their material benefits.

The scent of hot coffee clings to the vapour escaping from the enamel pot on the polished stove, the Flemish peasant woman calls her husband and watches him rise shakily from his seat. Years ago he had a tram accident, but being too poor they were unable to pay specialists' fees. She is thankful that she is strong and able to take in washing. As they sit opposite each other savouring their simple meal, they talk about their son's new house, with an 'upstairs', the new school their grandchildren attend, the electric cleaner which has replaced the broom in their daughter's house. But there is no self-pity, no regrets, no envy. Just stubborn resignation and hope for their children's future. They are unaware that as their loved ones become numbers on index cards, or anonymous pairs of hands to manipulate the tools of modern industry, they will lose some of their self-respect and become like the grains of corn to be sown and reaped at the whim of market speculators. The price they will have to pay for progress and advancement will be to lose themselves in a coagulating mass easily moulded and manipulated by the powers of the day. Their heritage, the Dignity of Man, stripped of its meaning, will be like the weed in the field – the target for psychological weed-killers, by both political and giant corporations.

The old woman clears the table, gathering crusts to feed her rabbits. She has never heard of Tibet and is not even aware of a place called Norway. No one has ever told her about her spiritual affinity with her sisters. She plods about her work, resilient like the poppy which skirts the fields of golden corn. She bends to the storms and her seeds germinate in the muddy scars of tanks, rooting themselves in the blood-soaked earth where great armies met and fought in the senseless orgies punctuating the history of mankind.

Her work finished for the day, she retires for a well-earned rest. Uncluttered by the appendages of an acquisitive society and unruffled by 'social standings', she'll sit for a while by her gleaming stove, knitting or darning, never idle. Her children may reap the benefits of this materialistic society, but like the huge sea of golden corn, it is left to the little red poppy to relieve the monotonous uniformity of such wealth by distracting the eye of the onlooker to its tiny red cup as it bends and sways at the end of its slender green stalk.

Undemanding, unpretentious, the old peasant woman may be despised by some, or considered unprogressive by others, even accused of superstition, but she and her sisters are a glowing symbol of our global universal affinity with the creative powers and energies of Mother Earth from Gaia to the dance of Shiva...

13

'We've got no Doggy'

The bucket grated on the stone shaft of the well and came to an abrupt halt on reaching the water. In the lull as it filled, Jill sighed irritably. Her blue eyes filled with hot tears of frustration and her round cheeks flushed as she wound the chain and leaned over to grab the swinging bucket.

'Now just you come with me,' she called to her small son, whose features were unrecognisable under the thick coating of freshly mixed concrete. 'It was very naughty to play with Daddy's concrete. He needs it to mend the kitchen steps.'

'Doggy take care of Daddy's things,' gurgled the child as the cold wet flannel was whisked swiftly round his face.

'We've got no doggy!' Jill snapped as she plunged his arms into the water and swilled them down. 'It's time you grew out of this imaginary game. Everything that disappears is "Doggy's" doing! Well, I know it's you, and...' But the clatter from the kitchen cut her short. 'Oh dear,' she sighed, 'now Daddy's fallen over the tool box I left out...'

Steven's oath reached them, a little muted. Then he called out, 'Jill? Jill, where have you put today's mail?'

There was a pathetic ring in his voice, like a small child on the verge of desperation.

87

'I can never find anything in this house!'

'I think it's on the table under the wallpaper,' she suggested quickly.

'No, I've looked there. In fact I've looked everywhere it shouldn't be!'

'Then try looking where it should be.'

'Not there either. It's important, Jill. Do try and be helpful.'

'Helpful?'

The hysterical note in her voice made Steven look out of the kitchen window.

'Oh Henry!' he moaned, winking as he caught the grin on his son's silent face. But on seeing the light of battle in his wife's eyes, he retreated as gracefully as he could with a mild 'Never mind, dear, I'll find it...'

For the second time Jill heard the grating of the tool box as Steven stumbled over it. But no oath followed and when she entered the kitchen it had been moved aside.

'Off to bed with you!' she snapped, as she pushed her son up the first few steps of the bare wooden stairs. 'And stay there until I call you.'

She returned to the well, this time for water for their coffee, and once again sighed, 'I must try to calm down.'

She looked so tired as she sat slumped over her steaming mug that Steven refrained from trying to reason with her. Instead, he patted her shoulder.

'It'll be much easier when we have running water. If only that dealer would answer and maybe buy my collection, we could afford the tanks and pump and...' But he was cut short as the sounds from overhead told him that far from being contrite over spoiling his father's concrete, Henry had found his coin cabinet, and, tipping tray upon tray, was playing with Steven's precious coins.

'Oh, I give up!' cried Jill.

For a fraction of a second Steven hesitated between his wife's tears and rescuing his painstakingly collected pieces.

'Take an aspirin,' he suggested, as he took the steps two by two.

Too tired even to sleep, Jill lay in the dark, listening to the lonely call of an owl. Her limbs ached from mixing more concrete and her nerves were on edge from constant frustration. She realised sadly that she was being more unreasonable than her small son, but the more she tried to reason with herself, the tauter she felt. Like and overstreched piece of elastic ready to snap at any time.

Poor Steven! she thought sleepily. It would be such a shame to give up that collection just to get water ... I wish ... I wish ...'

Her thoughts turned into a dream as she slipped comfortably through the waves of darkening sleep, swallowed by the giant shadows of the tall trees at the edge of her moorland home as she stood surveying their ramshackle cottage. A faint smile relaxed her features as the gentle breeze carried the scents of the night to her through the open window. Ramshackle it may be, hard work, too, she thought. But it was *home* and one day it would look really nice and Steven would have a pleasant surrounding to work in and Henry would enjoy a healthy open-air life.

A sudden crash jerked her out of this pleasant dream. For a moment her heartbeat seemed to increase, as it does when one falls into nothingness at the twilight of sleep, and a rush of cold air brushed her cheek. She wondered if her nerves had at last snapped. Unconsciously she listened to the owl's lonely call and the nightingale's ode to the night, and the peace and calm she'd longed for engulfed her and somehow she felt convinced everything would be all right. It was the clatter of the tool box which awoke her a little later.

Poor Steven, she thought. I should have cleared away the tools . . . But she was suddenly aware of a snore which rose from the lump beside her.

'Steven,' she whispered, trying to shake him awake. 'We're being burgled!'

'Never in all this world! Who'd want to burgle this place? Be sensible and go back to sleep.'

But she was wide awake now, and searching for the matches. Once the soft warm glow of the oil lamp bathed the room, returning the weird dark shapes to familiar objects, she found her dressing-gown and started threading her arms into the sleeves.

'What have you put on the stove tonight?' she complained, as unpleasant fumes seeped in under the door.

'Maybe I forgot to check the flues . . . I'll go and see . . .' Steven fumbled sleepily for his sweater. 'Why do you always move things? I left it on the chair as usual.'

They sat on either side of the bed, aware of the other's thoughts after the search proved futile, and Jill remembered vividly the shadow which had brushed her cheek a while ago as the breeze had seemed to increase. She stared at the window, which stood wide open, whereas she distinctly remembered leaving it on the catch, halfway.

'I heard a crash earlier,' she started to explain. 'Maybe someone got hurt and they came for help or something . . .'

'"Or something" being the operative words!' Steven tried to make light of it, but he added in a lower tone, 'Or we have a burglar!'

Bent on surprising the intruder, he kicked open the kitchen door and rushed in, tripping over the tool box. He lunged forward, hands up ready for the impending collision with the back door, but it was ajar. He found himself staring down at the deep craters in his newly concreted steps.

'Damn!' he muttered under his breath. 'It'll all have to be done all over again ... There's a hoodoo on this place!'

He looked over his shoulder at the empty room where pipes, cement bags, plaster and tools received his protest silently as Jill's voice, not even carrying a note of surprise, welcomed the village constable.

Steven's eyes focussed on the heavy boots.

'We found the stolen car at the bottom of your lane and thought he might try your cottage...' Even the voice sounded heavy, with local accent if nothing else, thought Steven. 'Hello, here's a fine set of prints if ever I did see one!'

The big man stooped slowly before kneeling down by Steven. Together they contemplated the concrete steps in silence for a while.

'He's a killer,' the constable confided in a whisper. Then, sensing Steven's stiffening, added a trifle too casually, 'There's a fat reward for his capture, I'm told.'

From the other side of the yard came a deep, menacing bark.

'Your dog seems to have found the scent...' said the constable.

'We've got no dog,' retorted Steven, still smarting over his spoiled work.

Then he remembered the giant marks which had originally spoiled his efforts, and Henry had proudly stated it was 'Doggy'. He had been on the verge of demonstrating to his son that it didn't pay to blame

91

imaginary dogs, far better to be honest and admit your guilt like a man, when Jill told him small children often made up imaginary pets and play-mates. 'OK. So it's Doggy,' he'd answered curtly. 'But tell Doggy you'll be punished next time he does something naughty.' And next time Henry hadn't tried to blame the dog. He'd been caught covered from head to toe in newly mixed concrete.

He remembered the light of battle in Jill's eyes, and was beginning to understand a little how she'd felt that morning. Poor Jill, he thought, if only we had running water...

The dog kept up his barking until the constable laughingly rose and, adjusting his tunic, said with broad, heavy humour, 'No, sir, I see what you mean. It's more like a donkey. A Great Dane, is he? Well, let's see what he's found.'

Steven was about to protest but remembered in time the hint of a reward.

'OK,' he laughed. 'What have we to lose? And, what's more, that rogue has my best working sweater.'

They skirted the barn in the dog's wake, trampled over the rickety bridge by the old mill and went on towards a derelict cottage.

'That was Miss Jenny's,' the constable informed him, as an excuse for calling a halt. 'Some say she put a curse on the place. Weird noises are sometimes heard at night, and there's those who swear they've seen shadows or a ghost! She had a powerful temper and they say that when they come fetch her body it was sitting bolt upright, staring straight at them with fire in her eyes. She'd poisoned herself after the council took her pets away.'

'Well, there's someone living there now. Look, the path is well trodden and there is a lump of fresh concrete...' Steven stopped dead as the thought struck him. 'From my steps! Come on, constable, what are we waiting for?'

Jill's eyes questioned him silently as she watched him light his pipe.

'He gave us no trouble,' said Steven, complacently. 'He burned his shirt in our stove because it was blood-stained, and was about to make his get-away in our van...' There was a queer smile lighting up his features which Jill couldn't identify. 'Until he was frightened away by that dog, one of Miss Jenny's pets, no doubt!'

She waited.

'Well?' she reluctantly asked as Steven remained silent.

'Well?' Victory spread like wildfire over his features. 'You should see old Miss Jenny's cottage! Our missing tools. Tins, loaves, bones...'

'He was probably hiding out there.'

'With my lost slipper, my pipe, my bills.' He was gratified by her expression. 'Yes, dear, my bills and my mail. Including the letter I was waiting for from that dealer.'

'But you have the reward coming to you.' Her voice sounded like music to him. 'There's no need for you to sell your coins any more.'

'And you'll have running water just as soon as I can fix that tank and the pump. And I'll get a generating motor ... As soon as it's daylight I'll take the van and get the stuff myself.' He followed her eyes as she gazed at the ball of fire rising over the edge of the moors. Then the stampede on the bare wooden stairs made them turn to see their small son rush to the back door.

'Good Doggy!' cried the child wildly. 'Doggy looks after Daddy's things ... He knows good hiding place...'

With concrete still stuck to his pads, the Great Dane entered, proudly carrying Steven's sweater. With great dignity he allowed Henry to pat him before looking down at the beaming little face and licking it gently.

'It must be one of the pets who got away when they took Miss Jenny's dogs...' mused Steven, as Jill scrambled eggs for their breakfast.

It smelled good, and he felt incredibly hungry after his night's work.

'Ah!' he said with satisfaction, holding out his hands as she heaped a great helping on a plate. But his anticipation was frustrated as he watched her, speechless, place the plate on the floor.

'Important guests first,' she smiled, and her features seemed unusually bright as the light from the strengthening sun bounced off the bright tap.

Soon it would no longer be an ornament ... And Steven was convinced the guest had come to stay!

14

The Lady of the Lake

The noise from inside the Grand Hotel mounted in a crescendo as the party came into full swing. The clinking of glasses, the chatter and laughter sounded not unlike the crashing cymbals of the orchestra. A few couples strolled among the gardens which swept down towards the lake.

'Alone, on a night like this!' exclaimed Helen Chatterton, the rich young widow who was acting as hostess. 'Aren't you enjoying the party? Such a brilliant gathering, and all in your honour!' She rested her heavily ringed fingers on the parapet of the balcony, and the jingling of her many bracelets clashed unpleasantly with the tempo of the music.

David Spencer shuddered involuntarily. He had come to the balcony to enjoy the sweetly scented fresh air of this late May evening and resented the intrusion. He had never liked Helen, in fact she had spoiled his friendship with Mark Chatterton. Mark was born for success, and she had homed in...

'Why the silence?' she asked again. 'Aren't you enjoying your big moment?'

'Yes,' he answered hesitantly, 'of course I am...' He was aware of a slight movement but was too slow to avoid the contact as she threaded her hand through his arm.

She would be smiling, he knew; her wide red mouth stretched, revealing her immaculate white teeth, false, he was sure. But he didn't look at her, wishing desperately that it could have been Mark at his side now that the world was at last acclaiming his work, ending the frustration of those long shunned years. They had studied together, hoped and dreamed together, and success should have come to them both together.

As it happened, Mark had produced a gaudy, noisy, but shatteringly successful musical which paid for his indulgence in his wife's expensive tastes; and killed him!

'You know how it is,' he had laughed spilling the notes on the table as he bought the expensively fast car Helen had always wanted. 'Women love being indulged, and I'll get as much fun out of it. Wait and see if you don't do the same when your turn comes...'

David remembered the noise of that engine as Mark drove off in a hurry. That was the last time he had seen him alive. And there, in the gravelled yard of the Grand Hotel stood that infernal machine, Helen's pride!

The silly chump, thought David. He should have banked his money...

'I'm so proud of you tonight, David.' Helen's voice cut in on his reminiscences.

He sighed. At least she helped him enjoy his life, I suppose, he thought philosophically, and maybe that helped him to be successful.

'You seem miles away,' she was teasing gently. 'Have you heard a single word of what I said?'

'Yes.'

'Well, let's get back to the ballroom, you owe me a dance.' She tugged at his sleeve, urging him into action. 'You're famous now, David. All the society hostesses will want to ask you to their parties...'

So, that's it! thought David self-pityingly. The curse of

success! When empty-headed females drag you in public, clinging to your sleeves to show off their latest prize as a slap in the face to their rivals! How could Mark stoop so low?

'I'm sorry,' he faltered, brushing off her hand, catching his finger on one of her expensive rings, 'but I'm no good at dancing.'

'Nonsense, you dance divinely!'

'Well, right now I have other things on my mind.'

'I know the signs.' Undaunted and self-assured, she steered him skilfully down the steps leading to the velvety lawns. 'Mark used to get a little moody when he was composing. Come, let's row on the lake. Such a lovely night, and they say the lake is haunted when it's a full moon. That should help inspire you.' She gave him a quizzical side glance. 'Or at least interest you.'

David rowed to the middle of the lake before letting the boat drift pleasantly and silently. The air was fresh and moist with dew, the soft lapping of the water against the boat, soothing. The only movement in this stilled setting seemingly the tiny fragments of the moon dancing around them gaily as if in an attempt to please. He started humming a tune to the tempo of their dance, oblivious of Helen's presence. The dance grew livelier and his tune stronger, echoing back pleasantly from the trees along the banks of the lake, almost calling him by name, he thought.

'Is that going to be an aria for your new opera?' asked Helen.

Her voice broke the spell. He pulled himself together. 'Might be.'

'Working on it already? I thought you were going on holiday...'

'It has to be submitted by the first of November.'

'That gives you under six months.'

'Once the characters are clear in my mind the rest falls into place.'

'The trouble with you is you create these puppets so vividly they become more alive to you than the real people around you. Mark never made that mistake.'

There was reproach in her voice and when he looked at her he thought he could detect a slightly pained expression. He had resented her intrusion into his privacy but, he suddenly thought, that did not excuse him from behaving like a bore!

'I'm sorry, Helen,' he said on impulse. 'There are times when one almost feels compelled to act in a manner completely out of one's control, as if drawn by some unknown force. Tonight I suddenly felt as if someone was beckoning me ... You must think me very ungrateful.'

'You sound as if you almost expect your creation to materialise!' She quickly checked her outburst, and added softly, 'You work too hard ...'

'You think it mad, don't you,' he stated.

She bent forward and rested a hand on his knee. The touch wasn't unpleasant; it conveyed warmth, almost sympathy.

'Don't dwell on it any more. You know you can always rely on me for comfort and support. I could do so much for you, David,' she murmured emphasising her words with a slight pressure of her manicured fingers.

She was smiling, and the moonlight bounced off her white teeth harshly. David only saw greed in their sharpness, and the lust for power in the moist dark eyes overshadowed by the heavily mascara'd eyelashes. Worse, he saw what he took to be blood on the varnished nails, like the claws of a bird of prey holding on to its kill. She was bending forward, bringing her face to within inches of his, but just then the voice of the lake rang out, calling him by name: David ... DAVID ... David! It was as if each ripple picked up the sound and tossed it to the next until it became a mere whisper and finally died away in the depths of the lake itself.

David stood up suddenly, rocking the boat dangerously, with Helen plucking at his sleeve as she tried to restrain him.

'Let me go!' he cried sharply, pushing her down roughly. 'I must go.'

He could hear her calling him back as he swam through the moon-drenched lake. The coolness was exhilarating, the softness of water as it passed through his fingers and caressed his face was sheer delight. He laughed, the sudden sense of freedom had recaptured his lost youth.

Through the distorted shadows reflected in the broken mirror of the lake Helen had the illusion of watching two people in gay abandon. Their laughter and happiness, a challenge to her, cut deeply into her pride. Never before had she failed to get what she wanted. Never before had any man resisted her, let alone plunged into a lake to get away from her!

Locked in her room, her face ravaged by tears of frustration and anger, she planned her revenge. By morning she was cool, and on the attack, but she allowed David to make his apologies, enjoying with some satisfaction his discomfort.

'I just don't know how to explain...' He faltered, turning away from her crushing stare. 'I suppose it was mad of me...'

'Last night I only thought you were mad,' she said, cuttingly interrupting him, 'Now I know you are. I had heard rumours about your eccentricities but I draw the line at ghost hunting! Imagination is one thing, but when it gets out of hand it needs a strong person to keep it in check.'

'And no doubt you think you qualify...'

'You have little choice! A little embellishment on my part and this story would convince your family once and for all that you really *are* mad. At least, married to me you'd have security and position...'

He had come in remorse, ready to make amends for his boorish behaviour; now he knew it had been a waste of time. 'Now look here, Helen, I don't love you. Wild horses wouldn't drive me to marry you! What's more, all you're in love with is power and money ... All you want is success.'

'Which I would have. Your success, power over you – the money I already have.'

'This is where you come unstuck!' David cried triumphantly. 'Is this the way you trapped Mark? I often wondered what he saw in you...'

Blind with anger, he stormed out of the room, only to find his path cluttered with reporters and cameras.

'Can you tell us more about your wedding ... name the day? Mrs Chatterton gave us an interview. Your idyllic night on the lake is front page news...'

He brushed them aside roughly without a single word and revved up his old MG noisily to drown their clamour.

After a few miles of fast driving he reached the brow of the hill overlooking the other side of the lake. The rising sun lay level, blinding him momentarily so that he almost missed seeing the girl cyclist pushing her twisted bike. Something about her frightened face as she looked over her shoulder when she heard him approach arrested his attention.

'Can I help you?' he called out as he overtook her.

He parked the MG on the verge of the road and

turned back, but the road was clear. He walked a few paces to the edge of the cliff where a narrow path had been cut by local fishermen.

'Marion!' he called out. The name had escaped him involuntarily and he looked dazed when a small boy appeared.

'Looking for someone, sir?'

The boy was struggling up the last few feet, clutching his catch proudly.

'No, thanks ... Jut stretching my legs,' he answered lamely. Digging his hands deep into his pockets he made for the car.

For a moment he sat smoking his cigarette thoughtfully. It had been on a morning like this when it had happened. The sun lying low over the brow of the hill had blinded him. He hadn't seen the girl, all he could remember was her twisted bicycle lurching through the air before his car plunged after it over the cliff. They never did find out her name when they recovered her body from the lake, but among her belongings was a gold bracelet engraved with a single name: Marion.

Life, as he had predicted when he reluctantly admitted defeat and married Helen, was quite unbearable. His only refuge, his study. There he found relief in his work, emerging only under duress. There was no time for rowing or swimming, but the foundations of the old house were lapped by the waters of the enchanted lake. They fed the creeper which clad it and David never tired of listening to the rustle of the breeze through the leaves which framed the window of his study. the balmy scent of the open blossoms seemed headier than usual as he stood by the window, gazing across the lake. He picked one, inhaled its fragrance, and its petals brushed his lips he was instantly aware of a sensuous sensation of sheer pleasure.

'Marion, oh Marion!' he whispered. 'Just a little longer and I'll join you, I promise.'

He made a habit daily of filling his study with the fragrant blooms, talking to them whenever he paused in his work, until one day Helen asked him, 'Who is this Marion I hear you talking to these days?'

'The only woman I have ever loved,' he answered calmly.

'Where does she spring from? I've never met her...'

'In the lake. In the creeper ... She is everywhere. She is the creeper!' he almost shouted in his exasperation at her questions.

The next day Helen had the creeper cut down.

'It were as if someone 'ad bin 'urt,' complained the gardener. 'It were like a 'uman cry, missus, when I tore it down.'

'Don't be stupid,' protested Helen angrily. 'Creepers are a menace.'

'But the Master, he hear it too,' persisted the old man, 'and he was really pained.'

Torn by grief, David lay in bed, tossing restlessly, tormented by nightmares he couldn't share.

'He is hallucinating,' commented Helen when the doctor arrived.

'High fever often produces these symptoms,' he reassured her. 'But you should have called me in sooner. Only a severe shock could have brought on such a relapse.'

'I don't understand. A relapse from what?'

'Some years ago he had a bad accident and suffered severe concussion and loss of memory. He seemed haunted by the girl cyclist involved. She was drowned and no one was ever able to trace her family. However, I think he may have been overworking and will need plenty of rest.' He gave Helen a meaningful glance. 'Make sure nothing upsets him.'

David recovered quickly under her careful super-vision, and life was assuming a pleasant pattern as she made a tremendous effort to please him. But the strain was beginning to tell on her by the time the autumn gales raged around the old house by the lake. Shutters banged, doors and gates creaked, and even David's calm got on her nerves.

From the warmth and safety of their living room she watched him take his first walk to the village post office. She had refrained from opposing him and suggested laughingly he should bring home some crumpets to toast by the fire. She watched him, bent against the wind, as he disappeared down the lane and suddenly felt lonely and afraid in this creepy old house. She realised she had grown fond of him, dependent on him for companionship. Forgotten was the nagging, the frustrations, the bitter jealousy, and it was with genuine warmth and pleasure she greeted him home.

'That walk did you good,' she remarked as they sat by the fire. She felt safe and secure now, able to ignore the howling wind which shook the shrubs until their branches rapped on the window-panes, the bare twigs looking like so many plucking fingers.

'Yes,' admitted David, 'I feel like a new man, now that the opera is finished. But I wonder if I shouldn't have done better to go to town and deliver it personally. They said at the post office there might be delays, the main road is flooded.'

A sudden crash made Helen jump. A limb from the old tree had torn a great gash in the roof.

'Don't worry,' David reassured her, 'I'll cover it with the old sail. Call the builder in the morning, they'll soon fix it.'

He had nearly finished when a vicious gust dislodged the loosened tiles about the hole. Trying to avoid them, David lost his footing and grabbed out for the chimneystack, but years of neglect had nibbled away at the cement, and the weakened masonry finally crumbled into the raging lake.

Early next morning, the First of November, bedraggled and wet, David Spencer was seen to enter the agent's office and leave again, disappearing into the driving rain. On the desk lay the wet and muddied MSS and scores, pleased it had arrived on time, he took the bus.

One stop from the village, he got off the bus and started to walk. There was no hurry now, the opera was safely delivered, time was at last on his side. He reached the brow of the hill overlooking the lake, a young girl cyclist got off her bicycle and started pushing it up the hill.

'Can I help you?' he called out.

She turned her head and looked over her shoulder, fear in her eyes, then a flicker of recognition sparkled and she smiled as the rain glistened on her wet cheeks.

His hand was wet as he laid it on hers and they laughed. Droplets of rain studded their faces before colliding and fusing into a liquid sheet. As they walked down to the lake the driving rain curtained them from view.

Back at the house, the telephone was ringing insistently. It was David's agent. 'I've scanned through his new opera, *The Lady of the Lake*. It's out of this world, Helen. I must speak to him. Its his best work yet!'

'Sorry,' replied Helen flatly, 'David was killed in the gale last night. They are searching the lake for his body right now.'

15

The Cricket

Lin and his older brother, Chang, lay on the banks of the little stream which flowed a *li* away from their village. Their small hands disappeared below the silver-sprayed corrugated surface of the swiftly running water, and dangled limply among the weeds. It was warm, and a stray cricket chirped in the background. Lin was close to dozing when Chang's cry startled him: 'I've got one, I've got a fish for our meal...' He held up the silver-blue and greeny-gold drop of rainbow which struggled resentfully from his fingers. 'Come on, Lin, you haven't caught anything yet!' he challenged.

The cricket stopped chirping, and Lin's drowsy eyes clouded with hot tears; he would have to return empty-handed... He buried his face in the cool grass. The only place which did not seem scorched was this tiny ribbon of weeds along the stream. The summer crops had failed, and everyone in the village of Liang Ts'un was on the rampage for food. Strangers came, and went, leaving tales of devastation and unknown diseases. As he opened his eyes, he saw the cricket; it stayed a few inches above his nose, resting on a blade of grass. It seemed to laugh at him, chirping as it rubbed its hind legs against its wings. Then it hopped away.

When they reached home the sun had dropped

behind the hills, enticing the light away with it and pulling a dusky pink blanket over the world. They noticed the windows were boarded, and the family's sacred amulet hung on the door; they dismissed it, anticipating the exclamations of the family as they handed their contribution to the evening meal to Ah-fang, their mother. But they were greeted in silence...

'What's wrong?' demanded Chang, cross, and disappointed.

'The sickness has entered our neighbour's house,' said Lee, their father.

'Father has hung up our sacred amulet to ward off the evil spirits,' added Ah-fang.

'Yes, we saw that. But how can it do that?' asked Lin.

'Tomorrow father will get you all amulets,' went on Ah-fang. 'You must not go outside without wearing one lest the evil spirit should enter you!'

They sat in silence for a while, dreaming of the open scorched fields and the rushing streams where it was so pleasant to lie and dip one's hands in its refreshing ripples.

'It feels like a prison in here, grumbled Chang. And Lin nodded, thinking how much he wished he were that cricket he'd seen that afternoon.

As if his thought had been transmitted to Jasmine, his sister, she asked: 'Grand-father, is it not said to be lucky to have a cricket in the house?'

'Very.' The old man nodded his head, then chuckled softly. 'Young ladies think that if they put one under their pillow, it will sing them to sleep, then they hope to dream of their future husband.'

'I wish I had one,' said Jasmine dreamily, wishing that by some luck they would be released from the epidemic.

'Would you like me to get you one to put under your

pillow, so you can dream of your future husband and hope he's handsome.' teased Lin.

Jasmine blushed and rose with surprising composure. 'No thank you, Lin. Mother said we were not to go out as we have no amulets.'

'Dare you ...' whispered Chang in Lin's ear. 'Bet you're too scared of the evil one ...'

'What does he look like?' asked Lin under his breath.

'Huge and horrid, with curly teeth and a tongue of fire ...' Chang laughed. 'When it is dark he lights up the countryside with flames coming out of his eyes ...'

Lin shuddered, and Chang laughed heartily.

When the household was soundly asleep, Lin crept quietly out of the house. At least I will have good warning of the evil one, if his tongue is of fire and flames come out of his eyes. I should see him from a long way off ... These thoughts ran through his mind as he made for the narrow green ribbon by the stream where he'd seen the cricket. But once he got there, and there was nothing more to do but sit, waiting, listening, he began to tremble.

Then he heard the cricket, and followed it, getting nearer and nearer till at last he held the struggling insect in the palms of his small damp hands. He could hardly breathe with excitement. He had not thought it would be as easy as this! Perhaps the evil one is asleep, he reflected, after all, Ah-fang was not in the habit of deceiving, yet there had been no signs of spirits ... A twig snapped, and he stood still. A noise like that could easily awaken a spirit, he thought, and he felt so helpless now that his two hands were cupped round the cricket. He moved more cautiously till he reached home, then pushing the door open with his toes, he slid quickly inside, and leaned against the familiar surface. 'Oh! That was dreadful...' he sighed. 'But now I must get you a jar, then you can start working...'

He carefully placed a sheet of rice paper on top of the jar and crept back towards his bed. The cricket started chirping, and he felt overwhelmed with joy; now all their troubles would soon be over.

Just then a huge shadow loomed up in front of him, and he gasped.

'Whatever's going on? What's this noise?' asked Lee sleepily.

'Oh father!... Nothing, I am just going to my bed.'

'How did that cricket get here? Lin!' Suddenly Lee realised what had happened, and he ran to the jar. 'We must get rid of it! No one must ever know you went out without your amulet...'

'But father!'

'Your disobedience is an ill omen.'

'But they bring good luck!'

'Have I not hung our sacred amulet on the door? This is a lack of faith in its powers...' He tipped the jar in the courtyard, then hurriedly closed the door. Lin could not bear to watch his cricket go; he ran to his mat, buried himself underneath it and sobbed himself to sleep.

By noon the family was convinced he had succumbed to the disease as he still had not emerged from his hiding. On one occasion he had peeped out and caught Lee's glance, a silent reproach which made him curl up and groan, almost convincing himself that he had the sickness, his stomach was twisting so ... When at last he got up, the children marvelled at the efficiency of the family's sacred amulet, to which they attributed Lin's swift recovery. Ah-fang secretly felt that his youth had probably something to do with it. Only Lee knew the truth, and he kept silent.

Outside, in the courtyard, the cricket rested on a twig.

'Look!' exclaimed Jasmine. 'There is a cricket in the yard.'

'That is lucky,' stated their grand-father.

'I will get it,' shouted Chang.

'No, you haven't got an amulet,' Ah-fang reminded him.

'Let me have yours, father,' demanded Chang impatiently.

Lee looked at Lin, and his silent reproach melted into a smiling understanding. 'I think Lin should get the cricket. His quick recovery has upheld the honour of our family's sacred amulet, and strengthened our faith in its powers.' And he placed his amulet round Lin's thin neck.

As he placed the cricket, HIS cricket, into the special wicker cricket cage his father had placed on the table, Lin felt like weeping with gratitude, and as the cricket chirped, he thought it sounded just like a laugh.